Praise for *Ida Mae*

"It is a unique coming of age novel in that it covers two generations—that of Ida Mae herself and that of her son, as well as the experiences of many of their friends. [The author does] an excellent job of switching midstory from one narrator to another who relates their own stories. [The] novel is fast moving and will no doubt hold the interest of the reader. As a storyteller myself, I appreciate that *Ida Mae* allows the reader to use his or her own imagination by not getting bogged down with [too much] detail."

—Madelyn Rohrer, Author, Member of the National Storytelling Network, the Lost State Writers Guild, Virginia Writers Club, and the Appalachian Authors Guild

"Mr. Taylor paints a diverse and inclusive cast of characters in Ida Mae's story. From a father who doesn't talk much to a neighbor with proven psychic powers and an ugly musician with a big heart and a hair trigger, . . . Ida Mae will take you far from home and back in the latter decades of the last century. Through grief and praise, and onward with the next generation, her coming-of-age story might call to mind your own. Enjoy both."

—Jon Howe, Author of *Shanghaied*

Ida Mae: And Her Passage to Chautauqua
by Rick Taylor

© Copyright 2024 Rick Taylor

ISBN 979-8-88824-271-1

All rights reserved. No part of this publication may be reproduced, stored in a retrieval system, or transmitted in any form or by any means—electronic, mechanical, photocopy, recording, or any other—except for brief quotations in printed reviews, without the prior written permission of the author.

This is a work of fiction. All the characters in this book are fictitious, and any resemblance to actual persons, living or dead, is purely coincidental. The names, incidents, dialogue, and opinions expressed are products of the author's imagination and are not to be construed as real.

Published by

◤ köehlerbooks™

3705 Shore Drive
Virginia Beach, VA 23455
800-435-4811
www.koehlerbooks.com

Ida Mae

Ida Mae

And Her Passage to Chautauqua

RICK TAYLOR

VIRGINIA BEACH
CAPE CHARLES

To my wife, Shannon, who encouraged my writing and put up with my long absences as I sat in my office transfixed by my computer. The following poem is dedicated to her. Any acknowledgment should go to her as well considering the many reviews she willingly conducted.

A PIXIE FROM TEXAS

She has captured my soul
this pixie from Texas,
this enchantress
whose smile
always lifts me high
offering proof of her generosity
and caring.

I'm blessed
that she has chosen me
a struggling writer and poet
whose light has yet to shine.
Who can doubt
that her love and brilliance
will charge my engines
and change my water
into wine.

Part I

Chapter 1

Bridget and her daughter, Jess, lived in the holler, a place where Momma said I couldn't go even though Jess was my best friend, but I went anyway. After all, it wasn't Jess's fault that she lived in the worst part of town. As a single unmarried woman with no job, her mother couldn't afford to live anywhere else. Who was Jess's father? No one seemed to know, but some guessed it might have been the handsome salesman who came to town some thirteen years back. That guess seemed to be pretty good, too, since Jess and I are both thirteen.

Everyone noticed Jess's mother, Bridget, right off—an incredible figure, straight black hair, black nails, black lipstick, black outfits, and black eyeshade all contributed to the exotic look she seemed to favor. And she had that great name to go along with all of it. But I was *Ida Mae*, even though Jess and I knew that it was a stupid sounding name that pegged me as being right out of the coal fields. Why couldn't I have been given a classy name like *Bridget*?

Some townsfolk in the valley said Bridget was mysterious more than exotic, even frightening, considering her tall stature and piercing black eyes. Some even considered her to be a soothsayer or seer. In real early times, they probably would've called her a witch since she claimed to have the ability to foretell the future, but I never heard anyone use that term to describe her.

Only Jess and I knew about Bridget's trances. During one of them, Bridget not only advised Jess and me that Farmer Platter's prize pig had wandered off but also where to find it. I informed Daddy without identifying my source. Sure enough, the owner found the animal right where Bridget said it would be. Although Daddy was most curious, he never pressed me for details.

Bridget's gift dazzled Jess and me, but we never told anybody about it. Jess was too scared to stay around by herself when a trance was coming on, so she didn't have much more experience with them than I did. At first, we just sat there listening, but, by and by, we started noticing things—like with the Platter pig—that turned out to be true. And so, we started taking notes.

Anyhow, when I went to Jess's house one day to make cookies, Bridget was sitting on the sofa. Soon, her eyes started to roll back and her eyelashes began to flicker. Jess and I knew that in a few minutes she would sit bolt upright and begin spouting words as she looked straight at us without seeing us. We would be ready, pads and pencils in hand, to transcribe what we heard.

From experience, we knew that catching her words on paper wouldn't be easy. Bridget could spout about anything, including the weather, local gossip, farm prices, politics, and crime. The problem was, she usually talked as fast as a rabbit with its tail on fire and never gave us headlines. Well, soon enough, this particular day, her head popped up at an angle that gave evidence to a glazed look that always preceded her ramblings.

"Something incredible is going to happen at vesper services this coming Wednesday, and it will involve Loretta Looper."

And that's all she said.

The short pronouncement flabbergasted Jess and me. Typically, Bridget went on for fifteen minutes or more. Later, we decided that her subconscious must have spotted our notepads and got gun-shy. One thing was sure as ketchup, though: Neither one of us was going to miss that vesper service.

The night before the service, it snowed. There's nothing prettier than Mammoth Falls, West Virginia, when the snow's up. When it gets in the trees and on the houses, it looks like a Christmas card, and with the full moon blazing, a purple tint comes to it all that never fails to take my breath away. The town is in the woods pretty much, except where trees have been cleared away for some structure or other, usually a single-family home.

I can't remember whether the moon was up that night, but I do remember that Daddy showed up early from work and that almost never happened. As usual, at dinner he was wearing long johns under his overalls, and before we went outside, he added a flannel shirt, a mackinaw, plus a fur cap to cover his bald spot. Under a winter coat, Momma wore a long navy-blue velvet dress with a wide, white collar. She looked real pretty, too, though Daddy never said so. Daddy never talked much.

My younger sister, Patsy, and I wore our Christmas mittens with matching socks and scarves topped by fur-lined canvas jackets over blue jeans and leather boots. Both of us had ponytails held in place by ribbons, hers pink, mine blue. Momma had instructed me earlier, "Ida Mae, you wear your green dress. It's time you shed those jeans," but I defied her, and she didn't have the heart or the time to argue, which wasn't like her at all. She was always saying things like, "Ida Mae, don't slouch, hold your back straight, wear a dress." The most interesting part was that Daddy didn't usually go to church on Sundays, let alone on Wednesday evenings for vespers. On the way to church, he gave his reasons for coming.

"Sure as ketchup, there's gonna be a healin' tonight. Wouldn't miss it fer the world."

That was all he said. Like I mentioned, Daddy never talked

much. Right then I knew what he meant. He must have found out that something special involving Loretta Looper would take place, which in his mind had to be a healin' since Loretta had Parkinson's.

I felt my Adam's apple getting hard and thought for a second that I would choke, but I held on. That Daddy would expect a healing was not surprising. In fact, that was exactly what Jess and I thought just as soon as we learned that Loretta would be involved. Most folks in our valley knew that Loretta had Parkinson's. The only logical conclusion was that any event involving her in church would involve a healing of her affliction. The next assumption would be that Reverend Highwater, our minister, would be the one performing the ritual. That was what Jess and I thought, and Daddy had the same hunch, I suspect.

The answer to the next question wasn't so easy to come by: How did Daddy find out about Loretta's connection to the vesper service? Sure as ketchup, it wasn't Jess or me what told him. We agreed to tell no one, not even Bridget, who never remembered anything she said afterwards anyway. We'd entered a pact of silence sealed with blood. We cut our thumbs with a pocketknife right then and there. We both knew that a blood pact was the most sacred pact there was and that it was forever binding, even unto death.

For the most part, I'd kept that pledge, too, except for a few members of our gang plus a couple of friends at Western Auto. All told I would guess I let about ten friends know, including Hooper Handley, the Bascom twins, Stubby Wolf, Billy Bob Wycoff, Sleeper Stimpson, Weeder Bascom, Frog Bishop, and a couple of others. That's an awful lot, I know, but I got a pledge with new blood from each one—at least, I think I did. How Daddy found out will always be a mystery to me, but if Daddy knew about it, everybody in the valley would know about it.

The valley folks had always loved Loretta Looper, and all had been crushed when her affliction became known. Everyone concluded that she was much too young and too pretty to have Parkinson's. In high school, she had been voted the prettiest girl in the entire school, and most folks held the view that she was the prettiest in all of West Virginia—the US even. It hadn't taken long before she started dating Willard Looper, the most popular young man in the valley—handsome, smart, tall, and gentle. Folks insisted that it was a match made in heaven. Soon enough, they got married. Folks in the valley always said that eighteen was the ideal age for that.

Then, things started to go bad for them. Willard was almost killed in a mining cave-in. Although he came away without a scratch, it had been a close call, real close. Later, a doctor who had determined that Loretta couldn't have children also discovered that she had Parkinson's. Well, not long after, Willard took off—no divorce, just told Loretta he couldn't take it no more. By that time, she could hardly walk without help. At the tender age of twenty, she found herself in need of a wheelchair. The disastrous series of events put Willard into a tailspin. One day, he disappeared.

Loretta moved in with her parents, who lived in the valley. The neighbors took turns bringing food and driving her to the hospital. Valley folks are good that way. Loretta vowed that she would remain faithful to Willard and would wait patiently for his return. Occasionally, she would see Frank Tolliver, but no one thought it was anything serious. One day, he showed up on his motorcycle and kept coming to her house despite Loretta's attempts to dissuade him.

She assured her family and neighbors that she and Frank were friends and nothing more. Frank was known to be wild and crazy, an unlikely match for Loretta, reputed to be as pure as the driven snow. Folks said she remained as sweet as ever despite all her bad luck.

The view around town was that the Lord had asked too much of Loretta. Take her husband or take her health, but don't take both. That's why valley folks had gotten so excited about a healing for her, and the idea wasn't too farfetched either.

You see, about a year ago, one of the valley folks, Iggy Parsons, was hunting rabbits when a snake bit him. Everyone thought he was a goner for sure when they found out it was a timber rattlesnake. It happened on a Sunday, and on the way to the hospital Iggy insisted on stopping at the Sunday service. When he appeared, Reverend Highwater stopped his sermon halfway through so he could wave his hands over Iggy while saying prayers and other incantations.

Iggy healed up good as new, and word got around. Now, everyone assumed that Bridget's prediction could only mean a healing for Loretta. Coming as it did, the storm of interest was to be expected.

When we arrived at vesper services, our tiny church was packed to the rafters. That contrasted vastly with past vesper services when you could roll a bowling ball down any row of seats without hitting but one or two. Knowing that my family would be late—they always were—I had Jess and Bridget save us seats in the row directly behind Loretta, who always came early with her parents. Eventually, all of us were spread out, with me on the aisle followed by Jess, Bridget, Momma, Daddy, and Patsy.

In the few minutes before service began, I studied Loretta. She was as beautiful as ever in her red dress. Her blond hair was pulled up, revealing a beautiful neck and two small ears, each adorned with a tiny gold hoop. When she looked to one side, she revealed a full set of red lips, the puffy kind favored by women in the movies. Then I noticed her wheelchair folded up at the back of the church, which prompted me to say a prayer for her. If anyone deserved a healing, it was Loretta. Then I saw Frank Tolliver sitting by himself in the last row, not far from the wheelchair.

The church showed off its Christmas splendor. On each side of the communion table stood a full-sized Christmas tree glowing with white lights. Two large wreaths had been hung on the chancel wall, one on the pulpit side, the other on the lectern side. Dark stained-glass windows gave evidence that there was no light coming from the outside.

Reverend Highwater sat in a chair close to the pulpit. He was obviously enjoying the organ music because his foot kept tapping in time to it. Momma had often said that if there was any man who looked more like God than Reverend Highwater, she sure would like to meet him—and marry him. Daddy would just laugh. Tall and handsome, in his mid-fifties, the reverend had long gray hair that he kept combed straight back. His hands were big as potholders, and when he began to wave them during a sermon while wearing his black robe, "he could preach the paint off the walls" as Momma often said.

Every unmarried woman in the valley was interested in the pastor when he first arrived. Then, he married a woman from Pittsburgh by the name of Samantha, and things quieted down a bit. Samantha made the difference. She always sat in the third row and had a way of bobbing her head when she sang. People sitting close to her said that she had a ghastly voice, but Samantha paid her detractors no heed. She was of perfect German stock, fair skin, blond hair, and German tough. Having been born in the States, she had no accent, but her family members, who visited frequently, made up for that deficiency.

As a singer, Loretta was just the opposite. The folks who sat near her agreed that she sang like an angel. When we started the first hymn, I could hear her voice. It was so soothing that I kept silent so that I could enjoy it. All the while, I could see various members of the congregation straining their necks to look at Loretta.

Next came the Old Testament lesson followed by another hymn, "Silent Night." The New Testament lesson was next. I knew Reverend Highwater would be in his pulpit real soon to deliver the sermon. All I could do was wonder about the healin', though. I could tell that Loretta was thinking the same thing. She was shifting in her seat. Like the rest of us, she was beginning to realize that the sermon would begin very soon. All present, including my family, began to realize that it would be a long walk home without a healin'.

Then Reverend Highwater sprang up and walked to the pulpit, where he stood like a giant. There were two white bands on his chest, attached to his white collar. The rest of his outfit was black. The light from the fixture inside the overhang shimmered in the pastor's gray hair. As always, he said a brief prayer before beginning, then he lifted his head.

At that moment, it happened.

You could hear a pin drop on cotton. The pastor looked toward the back of the sanctuary. By and by, we all craned our necks in that direction. And there, at the end of the middle aisle, stood a solitary figure.

Was it . . . ? Could it be?

"Hello, Willard," Reverend Highwater finally said. "Welcome back."

The congregation let out a collective gasp. Willard Looper, Loretta's long-lost husband, was standing under a light wearing a gray suit and red tie and looking very prosperous. *What a shame to be ruining that suit when they tar and feather him*, I thought. But nothing of the sort happened. People were too shocked to say anything against him or to move a muscle.

"Reverend Highwater, I've come for Loretta. I won't be leaving her no more."

The reverend paused before beckoning Willard to come forward. This was the church's big moment, and the pastor wasn't about to mess it up. Loretta was crying. Her shoulders were shaking. Without a second thought, Willard walked toward the front and stood behind the microphone on the lectern side. I held my breath.

Suddenly, all eyes moved from the front of the church toward the back again. We watched Frank Tolliver stand up and move down the main aisle toward Willard until he stopped right next to him. He removed an oversized handgun from his coat pocket, took aim, and shot poor Willard in the forehead.

Willard dropped like a puppet with the strings cut. The church fell deathly silent as the smoke from the single gunshot writhed upward.

Taking no chances on Frank Tolliver's further intentions, Reverend Highwater slid down behind the pulpit walls. In horror, we all watched as the gunman then put the weapon into his mouth and pulled the trigger. A loud report issued as his head disintegrated into sliced tomatoes.

Total pandemonium broke loose. I was too stunned to cry out, but Mrs. Meriweather, the choir director, screamed before fainting dead away. Her scream seemed to be a signal for every woman to join her in a show of earth-shattering frenzy.

Later, folks could only speculate that Frank Tolliver cared for Loretta much more than anyone suspected. Most likely, they thought, he developed a huge hate when he saw Loretta's husband appear just as he saw himself making headway with Loretta. The prospect of watching her fall back into Willard's arms was too much for him, at least that was what most folks in the valley seemed to say.

The most amazing part of it was what later happened to Loretta. Her Parkinson's went into remission. In fact, all symptoms seemed to disappear. The doctors said it was probably due to the shock of seeing two men she cared for fall dead on the church floor before her eyes.

Chapter 2

After what folks called "the vesper incident," they started buzzing like a swarm of bees. The murder-suicide was news enough, but when folks began insisting that Bridget had also predicted a healing for Loretta, all hell broke loose. Jess and I didn't have the nerve to report that Bridget had only said that "something special" involving Loretta was going to happen that night. A double killing without any healing at all would certainly qualify. But the valley folks insisted otherwise and wouldn't listen to our attempts to correct the misconception. Bridget was the beneficiary of their twisted view.

By and by, Bridget began to tell fortunes for money. Then, one of her "clients," Rachel, a beauty shop owner, offered to bring her in as a partner to tell fortunes at the shop. The idea was to combine fortunetelling with manicuring and hair cutting. *Come hear Bridget as she nails down your future. Hair what she has to say.*

It was awfully corny, I admit, but the folks in the valley seemed to respond to it. The women, especially, began streaming into the shop, and soon the men started coming. Before long, Bridget was making enough money to move out of the holler into a new house—rented, of course.

Bridget and Jess were very happy after that. Bridget even bought a TV, something we didn't own because Daddy said we couldn't afford it. With the newfound success, Bridget's appearance seemed to change. She replaced her straight black hair with something that Jess and I called a "vamp do." I wouldn't call it fantasy hair exactly, but it was moving in that direction—knotted on the top, swept-up, unruly. But she kept wearing her black outfits to preserve the mysterious mood.

When Bridget and Jess moved out of the holler and selected a house just three streets down from us, I didn't think Momma would have any further objection to my spending time with Jess. So, I was surprised when Momma continued to be upset about my visits. In time, though, I came to see that her negative views about Jess would remain no matter where Jess and Bridget lived. As far as Momma was concerned, Jess wasn't good enough for me. In her mind, she was "white trash" and that was that.

If the truth be known, Momma was always a bit snobbish. At first, I thought she was concerned that I was learning pagan ways, so I pointed out that Bridget and Jess never missed church, that they believed in God, and that Bridget's special "gift" was separate and apart from all of that. But none of that mattered to Momma. By and by, I overheard her talking to Daddy about Jess in a way that upset me greatly. They were at a place in our house where they thought I couldn't hear.

"White trash," Momma had called Jess, causing me to break the glass I was washing. I couldn't hear all the rest of it, but I got the gist. Momma was going to do her "damnedest" to separate us.

After that, Momma was always making up chores for me to do after school so I couldn't go over to Jess's house to watch television. Sure as blazes, I wasn't ready to give Jess up on account of Momma's wacky views. Instead, I got up real early in the morning to do the chores before school started and then skedaddled over to Jess's house when the final bell rang. Most often, Momma would just grit her teeth and bear it.

I don't mean to present Momma in a bad light. She was a good woman, an attentive and loving mother. It's just that she worried too much about me and my sister at times. She was always pointing out real good things about us both, though—like telling us that we'd be great beauties one day and complimenting our intelligence. Because of her, I'd been raised to be a good Christian girl who went to church every Sunday, and I was right proud of that.

Momma was the one who taught me about morals. She told me in no uncertain terms that no boy should ever touch my cooster, at least not until I got married. To that point, the boys hadn't ever even thought about touching my cooster, probably because they knew full well what would happen to them if they ever did.

Momma was kind of deceptive. At first glance, she came across as a frail little thing. She looked an awful lot like Dorothy's Auntie Em in the *Wizard of Oz*, and I often wondered how women her size could be so tough. She could tie all of us up in knots with just a look.

By spending so much time at Jess's house, I came to know Bridget's and Jess's likes and dislikes pretty well. One was just as superstitious as the other, with long lists of practices to be avoided—playing a piano during a rainstorm (they didn't even have a piano) or being the first to be buried in a churchyard (once you get that far, how much worse can it get?) or being rained on during a wedding or spilling water drawn from a well. They told me that a cock crowing in the early evening meant bad weather ahead and that your lover will be coming if you drop a tablespoon, and so on.

That's not even counting the superstitions that applied to Bridget's new business—cutting nails in regular order was a death omen; a crooked nail showed greed; black spots on the fingernails were a bad omen; yellow spots meant death. Girls who bit their nails would have a difficult time during childbirth; the larger the half-moon shape at the base of the fingernail the longer the lifespan; a person whose nails were cut on Sunday would be ruled by the devil all week, and so on.

Hundreds and hundreds of such superstitions abounded. I stopped trying to keep track. Truth was, Momma didn't have to worry none that I'd ever get tied up in such things. To me, the whole business was folly. Fortunetelling was something else, though. I never let Bridget tell me mine. I didn't want to know anything bad about my future. It scared me into fits just to think about the present.

So much can happen in just a few years. Momma says I went from being a beanpole to being a young woman overnight. I grew taller, yes, but that wasn't half of it. I also filled out around the hips and thighs. And in front, too—how can I say this delicately? My breasts grew dramatically, plus I grew insulation on my cooster.

Momma said that my period would come soon. I wasn't looking forward to that—no way, ugh! Even so, I liked what I saw in the mirror and the boys didn't seem to mind it either. The same thing was happening to Jess, although Momma said she wasn't near as pretty as me. That might be, but Jess was downright sexy in ways I couldn't ever duplicate, and the boys noticed that, too. She was not as big boned as I was, but she still filled out in front in a way that made me look puny.

The boys our age were starting to stare at both of us, but they looked like children next to Jess and me, plus they had those high-pitched voices. The same boys were still interested in playing jump the frog—or sticks and bones—whereas Jess and I were interested in other things—like older boys.

When they played old movies on TV, I'd stay over at Jess's on Saturday night to watch. Bridget would sometimes join us. At the time, she was going with a guy named Possum Winters who would sometimes stay for the movie, when he was sober, which wasn't often. It seems funny now that a viewing of *Citizen Kane* would represent an important point in my sexual rite of passage, but it did.

When *Citizen Kane* ended, I was sure that I'd seen something great. Here was a young man named Orson at the tender age of twenty-five playing Charles Foster Kane from early maturity to old age. His acting was spectacular. Bridget told us that a big tycoon named Hearst tried to squelch the film and that Orson had to fight that powerful man on top of everything else. I don't know how he did it all, but I suppose it was worth it since the movie turned out to be the greatest motion picture of all time, or so they say.

After the movie ended, we were talking about the word *Rosebud* when Bridget piped up that in real life that word meant something quite different from what the movie depicted. She told us that the term referred to one of the actress Marion Davies's personal parts. Jess and I got embarrassed because we both knew what part Bridget was referring to. That's when she asked if either of us had noticed any changes down there in recent months. Jess and I got to giggling. We were both embarrassed, but I sure knew what changes she was talking about. My cooster had been doing some funny things of late.

I explained that my period hadn't come yet, and Jess volunteered the same information, but Bridget said she wasn't talking about that. She said she was talking about a feeling—a good feeling—that made us want to touch that part. And that's how Jess and I learned about masturbation. The two of us later called it coostering, and I tried it later that night at home. WHOOOEEE.

Bridget told us some other things as well—like what happened to the male thing (she called it "the penis") when the boys got excited and how the sperm spurt out of it and where it was placed just before that happened. My mind was spinning, let me tell you. Bridget said we were coming to a turn in the road. There would be two ways to go. One way was to do what she would be doing with Jess. The other was to take a pledge of abstinence and stay chaste until our wedding day.

Bridget said that she intended to encourage Jess to take the pill so that she could have sex with as many partners as possible before marriage. Once married, Jess would then become "monogamous" (she explained what that meant) without wanting to experiment. Bridget told me there was plenty of time for Mom and me to decide which way I should go. Meanwhile, I listened to Bridget instruct Jess in the use of the pill.

The following afternoon, I visited Reverend Highwater at his office.

"Sex outside of marriage is a sin," he said. "You were correct to come to me about this, Ida Mae."

"Pastor, I've decided to take a pledge of abstinence before marriage. Still, I know what those feelings can do when they get started. I've felt them already. Despite my good intentions, I'm afraid that I'll be swept away. Shouldn't I take the pill, just to be sure?"

"There's nothing more beautiful than a woman and a man who come to the altar in a pure state. It's part of God's plan that they should do so. The pill will just tempt you to sin. It'll weaken your resolve."

There were other parts of the discussion, of course. I've just given the highlights. When I left his office, two things were firmly planted in my brain—first, that taking the pill was a bad idea and second, that all sexual relations before marriage were frowned upon. I didn't dare tell Momma about my conversations with Bridget or the pastor. She wouldn't understand. And when she later told me about the birds and the bees, I just let on like I didn't know a thing.

Then it happened. One day, I noticed a stain in my panties. At first, I thought it had come from a chocolate bar I ate that morning.

Then it hit me.

"Momma, is this what I think it is?"

She looked at the panties, then she looked up and smiled at me.

"Yes, dear. It's your period."

"Ugh."

"Ida Mae, you sit right down beside me on this bed. There are some things you should know about this important change in your life." She patted the bed.

"Oh, Momma, I know all about those things."

Then I sauntered out of the room. First off, I was somewhat embarrassed about the whole affair. Second, I was feeling kind of cocky. After all, I had had grown-up discussions both with Bridget and the pastor. Who could be more sophisticated than me?

The next month, I asked Momma a very telling question.

"Momma, on this period thing, can a person have a relapse?"

It was a beautiful spring. The trouble was, like the trees, my sap was building up in great quantities. On top of that, no matter how many times I went coostering, those feelings just didn't seem to subside. I felt like I was going to burst. By the time June arrived, we were set to do what Jess and I had been double daring each other to do since the weather changed.

The swimming hole was located on Platter Farm, out of view and surrounded by woods and shrubs. The older boys felt safe enough there to swim bare naked. We planned to hide in the thickets to watch. The difficulty was that we had to find a hiding place in the early morning, when no one was around, and then stay for hours until the boys arrived. Otherwise, the boys would spot us.

Good planners that we were, we took a lunch and settled in behind some bushes. By and by, the boys showed up. Soon, they commenced awhoopin' and asplashin' and arunnin' around. Well, each boy was different, that's for sure. But Sean Logan stood out from all the rest. WHOOOEEE. I got to wondering what Sean would look like excited, and Jess proceeded to tell me. By that time, she had been studying his talents up close. It was Sean who taught her about oral sex, and she, of course, had to tell me all about it. At the end, I was as hot as a Christmas goose.

That night, I got to do the math. I'd be sixteen in December, six months away. If I got married when I was twenty-one, I'd have to wait five years for sex. That meant that in sixty-six months or two hundred sixty-four weeks or 1,980 days, I would begin to experience what Jess was experiencing right now. Even if I coostered for only part of that time, it was sure going to be a lot of coostering. Right then I concluded that I'd better start thinking about marrying young, and in the interim before marriage, find a distraction to keep my mind away from sex.

Well, two things happened after that. First, I found a boyfriend. Second, I found my distraction. I'll start with the distraction. I was walking up a street a few blocks away from our house when I heard banjo music coming from one of the porches. Whoever was playing knew what they were doing. It began to go faster and faster, and as the pace picked up, I felt an urge to dance.

"Hey, you're pretty good," someone from the porch said as the music stopped.

"It's your music what done it," I answered.

"Come on up here, and I'll pluck you a few tunes."

That's how I came to meet Dodger. Oh, I'd known who he was. In a small valley town like ours, folks tend to know one another. It's just that I never shook his hand before, probably because he was so scary. He was big. I mean *big*—two hundred pounds, at least—and he had one of those buzz cuts that made him look like a prisoner of war. A stained T-shirt with no sleeves that was tucked into a pair of ragged coveralls was his outfit, capped off by bright-yellow hiking boots.

What with all his body hair, he looked like a gorilla—arms, shoulders, hands, neck, everywhere—topped off with a full beard. I put his age at about twenty, but he looked much older. Considering the weight, the short hair, and the ugly teeth—twisted and yellow in the front—I found myself, at first, spelling out *U-G-L-Y* under my breath, but then he began to play. As good as he was, all my negative thoughts just melted away.

I just couldn't stand still. Here I was in a calico dress sashaying around his porch in scuffed leather shoes. He kept playing, relentlessly. Well, right there and then I knew what my distraction was going to be. *I'm going to learn to play the banjo or die trying*, I said to myself.

"Dodger, can I ask you something?"

He'd stopped playing and pulled out a cigarette from his coveralls.

"Sure can," he said.

"Can you teach me to do that?"

"There's nothing to it."

"Except I'll need to practice, and I got nothing to practice with."

"No problem, Ida Mae. Go inside. In the living room, you'll find two more of these things on the sofa. Just pick one. You can borrow it."

"You're a wonderful man, Dodger, a wonderful man."

And so, I got hooked up with a banjo right then and there. Because Dodger was disabled from an Army wound, he was available every day after school.

Dodger told me I was a quick learner. By the third month,

I was playing complex tunes. By the sixth month, Dodger and I were playing duets. With a banjo, though, however good you get, there's always someone a lot better. I was okay, but I was a long way away from where he was, and we both knew it. Still, I was advancing. It didn't hurt that my sexual frustrations prompted me to practice for hours on end.

At the same time, I developed a relationship with Bleeder Thompson. His real name was Roy, but nobody ever called him that. The best thing about Bleeder was that he was safe. He was sixteen going on twelve with a voice high enough to prove it. Thin and gangly, he was kind of sickly looking. Awkward as he was, he was always bumping into things or falling, causing some body part, usually his forehead, to start bleeding, which is why his friends gave him his nickname, and it stuck.

Bleeder was the nicest, sweetest young man in the world. He wouldn't hurt a fly. He was soft-spoken, neat as a pin, and calm. Some people hinted that Bleeder was behind the door when brains were passed out. I didn't feel that way, not at all. Fact is, he got high grades in school, better than mine. He was no bell cow with people, that's for sure, but that was because he was shy. Best of all, Bleeder adored me, worshipped the ground I walked on. On top of that, he was flat-out afraid of sex. It took six months before he even kissed me. He was the perfect mate for someone intent on keeping her virginity until marriage, which I was. Trouble was, I had no romantic feelings toward Bleeder. None.

Between Bleeder and Dodger, I was seeing less and less of Jess, and I was happy about that as was my mother. To tell you the truth, I had gotten tired of Jess's sex stories. All they did was make me horny, and that was something I didn't need. But though Jess wasn't in my life as much, I heard a lot about her. Bleeder would fill me in on who she was doing it with on any given day. In place of "white trash" the word "tramp" sprang up in Momma's vocabulary. I did not hear it from Bleeder because he knew she was my friend, but I heard it from other people in addition to Momma.

By the time I was seventeen, Dodger and I were in a musical group playing on Friday and Saturday nights. Straight bluegrass it was, with us two on banjos along with a violin and a base. Dodger played guitar when needed, too. We called ourselves the Fun Pluckers. Bleeder came regularly to hear us.

Pretty soon, I had earned enough money from performing to buy a banjo of my own. Meanwhile, sexwise Bleeder and I weren't even close; a hand under the blouse was the extent of it. I was holding my own. Then, out of the blue, a new kid showed up in school. His real name was Hilary Richards, but everyone called him Wedge. I noticed him in class right off and the other girls did, too.

Handsome he was and sexy with jet-black hair. Where Bleeder was uncoordinated, this boy had the moves of a racehorse. Where Bleeder was thin and sickly, this boy was filled out, robust without being fat. I thought maybe he'd been held back in class, but that wasn't the case. He was smart as a whip, the son of a coal baron who had come to the valley to increase his fortune.

Well, I couldn't help flirting with him, and Wedge sucked it right up. Pretty soon, he was walking me home from school. Bleeder was furious. Still, he wasn't about to tangle with Wedge. Although I felt sorry for Bleeder, I couldn't stifle my feelings for Wedge. Momma picked up on it right away.

"He seems like such a nice boy, Ida Mae."

"Yes, Momma."

"And he comes from such a good family," by which she meant that he had gobs of money.

"Yes, Momma."

If she only knew. We were behind the Platter barn when it had happened.

"Ida Mae, you're so beautiful," he'd said.

"You really mean it?"

"Of course, I mean it." He smiled down at me. "Can I give you a sweet caress?"

"What's a sweet caress?"

"It's when I put my hand up under your panties."

I was stunned, but I didn't say *no*. He unzipped my pants and pulled them down to my knees. Then he had me lie down in the tall grass. WHOOOEEE! He had the technique of a brain surgeon. I got the distinct impression that mine wasn't the first cooster he'd caressed.

"Did you like that?" He pulled his hand away.

I answered him by asking him to do it again.

Then, as quickly as he had arrived in town, Wedge moved away. His father wanted to take charge of yet another operation in a far-off city. On the day of his departure, he walked me home.

"I'll never forget you, Ida Mae. You're all that's good about womanhood."

"Oh, Wedge, do you have to go?" I had tears in my eyes.

"You know I do. Someday, though, I'll come back for you and marry you. I promise."

(Years later, I would learn that Wedge died in a freak accident. He was sitting on the ledge of a window in one of the Yale dorms when he fell out. It was a tragic turn of events. I refused to believe it was a suicide and the paper didn't hint that it was.)

Not long after Wedge left, Bleeder and I were back together. By the time we were both eighteen, some amazing things started to happen. Bleeder matured. His voice changed, and he got to be fairly good looking. He must have sensed the change in my attitude toward him because, for the first time, he got the nerve up to put his hand you know where. WHOOOEEE!

After one of our makeout sessions, I began singing as I pulled up my pants. Bleeder told me I had a great voice and that I should sing on stage. When I tried the idea out on Dodger and the rest of the group, they gave me the greenlight. We started doing country and western hits at a spot called Sparky's. I was no Loretta Lynn, but still I was pretty good. What's more, I'd become a real beauty; at least that's what Bleeder, Momma, and Dodger all told me.

The crowd at Sparky's got bigger each weekend. Then the Jug Bar got wind of us and booked us for Wednesday and Sunday nights. We were on our way. By and by, someone from the music department of the University of Pittsburgh came along to hear me sing and play. Right afterwards, she offered me a full scholarship.

I was flabbergasted. I'd soon be a college girl.

Chapter 3

I ought to say a little about Mammoth Falls. First, there are no falls. Residents always wondered where the name came from and why it was called the "valley" when there was no valley. I learned that the Corps of Engineers or some such entity diverted a river that used to go through the middle of town. In the process, they closed off what used to be a "waterfall," but one that didn't qualify as being "mammoth" by any means. In fact, it was very small, not much more than a trickle. Still, the name stuck.

Memorial Day was a big deal in Mammoth Falls. One I witnessed stands out from all the rest. It was a beautiful, sunny day. The stores, shops, hotels, and bars were all closed. I'm not sure of my age at the time, except that I was very young. The image that comes to mind places me between my parents on Main Street. Even now, I can almost hear the pounding cadence of the approaching high school band.

Soon, high-stepping majorettes were in front of me, all with banners heralding the band's approach. I thought the majorettes were the most beautiful young women I'd ever seen. What's more, the marchers behind them were equally as perfect, obviously proud of their uniforms—red coats, high black caps worn low over their eyes, and shiny black boots. The band, dressed in identical uniforms, came by playing a tune I didn't know.

Next came young boys on bikes with red, white, and blue streamers lodged in the spokes. Weaving back and forth in front of me, they waved American flags. It was then that I noticed that the flag beside the local war memorial across the street was not at the top of the pole. When I asked my father about this, he told me that lowering the flag to half-mast showed reverence and respect for those who had died fighting for their country.

After that came firetrucks proudly driven by members of various local companies. Five or six of them passed by, all red and shiny. When one truck got close, Daddy asked where the Dalmatian was, a question that prompted laughter from the men in the front seat and from several people standing nearby. Momma later explained the gist of it—that Dalmatians were firehouse mascots. It took years before I saw a picture of my first Dalmatian in a magazine. I never could see what fire companies found so special about a white dog with black spots.

At the parade's conclusion, the mayor stepped up to a mic on the speaker's podium to introduce a large Black man to his left who was about to sing the national anthem. Daddy removed his hat as the song commenced. During the singing, I noted that several onlookers standing close by had hands over their hearts and tears in their eyes.

Back then, Vietnam was not part of my vocabulary. There wasn't even a thought of war. Still, that early memorial service was a forerunner, at least it was for me. Innocent as I was, I had no idea then that a war overseas would erupt years later, a war that would claim the lives of two men of significance in my life. Perhaps for that reason there was some process at work at some subconscious level, prompting my early fascination with my first Memorial Day parade.

I must admit that part of this memory may be a composite

formed from several years of attendance at such proceedings, but the initial template came from that first ceremony held when I was very young. Although I didn't understand all that the mayor was saying, I did understand a few words such as "honored dead" and "freedom" and "sacrifice" and "duty." I also noted the rapt attention of the crowd.

Then the mayor called upon the same man to sing what he called a "patriotic medley" accompanied by a "piano," except it wasn't a piano but rather a key-based instrument for use outdoors. Father explained to me later the songs he sang were "God Bless America," the "Battle Hymn of the Republic," and "America the Beautiful."

Next, a bugler from the high school band played "Taps." It was a very moving moment. Many onlookers began to cry. Even at my young age, I could tell that something very significant was happening. The mayor then called upon six participants wearing uniforms to fire their rifles three times as a tribute. The sound was deafening. The benediction, delivered by Reverend Highwater, ended the program.

We were walking home.

"Were those real bullets, Daddy?"

"No, Ida Mae, they were blanks. Real ones might hurt someone."

I sensed that Memorial Day had a lot to do with death, so I asked the next question.

"What happens after we die, Daddy?"

"No one can answer that, Ida Mae, although it is a very good question. Our own religion tells us that we go to heaven after we die. Even so, we come to that assessment by faith alone and not by any direct knowledge."

Chapter 4

I thank Aunt Ethel for my obsession with traveling. Each summer, she sent a check to my father, knowing that he didn't make much money working in the mines. Her purpose: to buy us a vacation, so long as she and her husband could come along. Having married well, she could be generous. With each check, she sent a note written in her shaky handwriting giving us details regarding the trip she had planned.

My father said each check included a "proviso," but as a kid I didn't know what that meant, and he didn't tell me. All I knew was that the check made it possible to travel with Aunt Ethel and Uncle Ralph to places like Niagara Falls or Williamsburg or Mackinaw Island or Gettysburg or Annapolis or New York City. My favorite designated spot was Chautauqua Lake.

The idea of traveling to a new place each summer got into my blood. I loved the adventure that came with it. For my parents, each trip was a bit of a strain because Momma disliked Aunt Ethel and Daddy couldn't stand Uncle Ralph. Because Aunt Ethel was short and stocky, Daddy was convinced that she had a Napoleon complex, telling me at the same time what that meant. Of course, my father agreed with Momma's views about Aunt Ethel, and she agreed with his views about Uncle Ralph. To Father, Uncle Ralph was a dufus, a man who would be "living in a hobo camp if he hadn't inherited a fortune."

Still, even with the tension, Aunt Ethel and Uncle Ralph provided a chance for me and my sister to get away on trips that Momma and Daddy couldn't otherwise afford. In hindsight, I can now see that my parents felt manipulated. Hard as it was for me to understand it then, I now understand why they were bitter about the arrangement. I also see that Aunt Ethel and Mom were in a power struggle regarding my father, a man whom both adored who reeked of integrity, was soft-spoken and gentle, a man who would cut off his right arm to help a friend or family member in need. Descended from Scotch Presbyterians, he was of pure stock, the kind of person who made this country great, not handsome by any means, but tall and muscular and honest.

As you might expect, he did fight overseas. In my mind as a young girl, he was the reason we won the war. Still, he didn't talk much, and Momma seemed to like it that way. With all his virtues, Daddy had two weaknesses—his sister and her husband. They could set him into a fury or a funk faster than any other known combination of people on earth. I remember one time when Aunt Ethel commenced talking about Daddy's lack of funds. We were on our way by foot to a movie theater in New York City

"You know you should save your money," she said.

He didn't answer.

She continued, "You never seem to have any. If it weren't for Ralph and me, you'd—"

"Can it, Ethel!" he said loudly.

We children knew that when Daddy raised his voice even slightly it was best to comply with his wishes. Aunt Ethel had apparently been taught from the same book because she clammed up immediately.

Momma was less subtle. She would tell Aunt Ethel off when her sister-in-law got out of line, which was often. Every year it seemed that the breach that occurred the prior summer would be too severe to repair; but then would come the letter and the check. Oh, I suppose there was more love than dislike there, and it's not that we didn't have fun when we were together.

Once in Annapolis, Uncle Ralph ordered the biggest batch of crabs he could find and took them back to the cottage, where we devoured them in short order. By and by, we were all dripping in butter. In the middle of our feast, Daddy noticed that the water was off. Apparently, a water line had broken in that part of the city. We looked at the mess in the room and at the grime on each other and burst out laughing.

In another year, we were having a wonderful time at a place called Keith's Kamp on Chautauqua Lake when Momma and Aunt Ethel suddenly discovered that the occupants in the cabin next to ours were chauffeurs on vacation. Snobs that they were, Momma and Aunt Ethel no longer viewed Keith's Kamp as a favored vacation spot.

During another excursion at Deep Creek Lake in Maryland, Momma and Aunt Ethel braved the hot sun while they rowed us to what they called "a secret place" on an island across the lake from our cottage. Once there, I was so excited about seeing fairies that I left my doll behind, an omission that wasn't discovered until we got back to our dock. The trip back in the hot sun put Momma in a fury, especially after Aunt Ethel backed out of the operation. As she rowed back over, Momma's fair skin turned bright red. In retrospect, I wonder whether it was sunburn or rage.

I'll always remember fondly the trip that Aunt Ethel planned to Washington, DC. Unknowingly, she scheduled it for the same weekend that the Freedom March was to occur. Luckily, Aunt Ethel was able to find rooms at the last minute, but she had to choose a second-rate motel, which to her was anathema. The day of our arrival, we followed a mass of people to the Washington Monument to hear a very inspiring speech delivered by Martin Luther King Jr.

"He's taking on quite a lot," Momma said afterwards.

"You bet he is, but he's up to the challenge," Daddy said.

"Even so, he's signed his own death warrant," Uncle Ralph added.

"What on earth are you talking about, Ralph?" Momma asked.

"The rednecks will kill him sooner or later," he said.

As it turned out, he was right, but it took five years for them to get up the nerve. Meanwhile, President Kennedy was assassinated by Lee Harvey Oswald in Texas. I suppose all Americans know where they were and what they were doing when they got the news.

On the day before it happened, Momma and I were eating lunch with Bridget and Jess at Phil's Fish Fry in Mammoth Falls. We got to talking about the president.

"He's such a hunk," Jess said.

"Trouble is . . . there's a lot of women ahead of you." I laughed.

"Jackie, for one," Momma said as she joined our laughter.

Bridget then made a comment. "Ladies, I'm extremely worried about this Texas trip. That's tough country down there. My gut tells me he's in danger, real danger."

Momma then responded, "You mean . . . ?"

"Yes, I have a foreboding that someone will try to kill him," Bridget said.

Of course, she was right. I later heard about the assassination on the radio and raced over to Bleeder's place to watch news coverage on his television. And I was watching it with him two days later, when Jack Ruby shot Oswald at point-blank range on live TV. What an incredible time! In the following year came the passage of the Civil Rights Act of 1964 announced by the president with the help of his Texas drawl.

Our family was having dinner at the local Howard Johnsons when the Tonkin Gulf Resolution was passed.

"Our crazy president has been hankering for a fight, and he's going to get one," Uncle Ralph said.

"Why, I don't believe that anything happened in the Tonkin Gulf at all. It's all bogus," Daddy said.

Of course, it turned out that they both were correct. Meanwhile, Johnson stomped Goldwater in the election by asserting that he would not escalate the war. By that time, Daddy didn't believe a word the man said. By the end of 1965, 184,300 troops were over there.

In 1965 came the march on Selma and the Watts riots.

Chapter 5

Nineteen sixty-six was significant for Bleeder and me. We were both eighteen and eyeing our nineteenth birthdays later that year—June for Bleeder and December for me. No way was Bleeder going to college. He didn't have any money. The draft board picked up on his status very quickly, making him 1-A as soon as they could. When he was directed to report for his physical, we decided to get married. It was quick notice, so the ceremony didn't have a lot of dazzle.

Reverend Highwater clamped one hand on Bleeder and one hand on me, said a few words, and declared us to be husband and wife. Bleeder was due to be off for basic training but not before we honeymooned at a local motel. We spent two nights discovering each other. When we finally had sex, it was wonderful, especially since we both knew that for each one of us it was the first time. By then, I'd gone on the pill—no sense taking any chances.

Then, Bleeder got his orders for Vietnam, and we both knew right away that he was in for a rough time. I wrote to him daily and worried about him constantly. In August, I decided to go to Bridget's beauty shop for a makeover, which I needed in the worst way. I also wanted to tell her about Bleeder and ask about Jess.

"It's so unfair, Ida Mae," Bridget said when I walked up to her.

"Bridget, what on earth is wrong?" I asked.

I noticed tears forming in her eyes as she continued, "It's Jess. She's dying. My baby's young life is being snuffed out, and it's all my fault."

"What are you talking about?"

"Jess developed a melanoma on her back. It looked like a regular mole. We thought nothing of it. Eventually, it became so pronounced we had a doctor look at it. By that time, it was too far along. She's in the hospital getting chemo right now. I know I'm being punished. I had to get away from the hospital for a short time and decided to come over here."

"Jess has cancer?"

"Yes . . . and there's no hope."

"Oh, Bridget, I'm so sorry. I didn't know." I paused. "But how can it be your fault?"

"As her mother, I wasn't a very good example. I encouraged her to have sex."

"Oh, fiddlesticks, Bridget! Jess charted her own course. She didn't need your help. Besides, by loving sex, she didn't set out to contract cancer. There's no connection. None."

I had trouble believing that anything bad would happen to Jess. I knew how much her mother loved her, and I loved her almost as much.

When Bridget offered to tell my fortune that day, I was reluctant. I was concerned that she would tell me something bad about Bleeder. By then, he was in Saigon. When I relented finally, she told me some good things about me, but when it came to anything about Bleeder, she clammed up. I could see right off she didn't like what the cards were telling her.

I said nothing as Rachel, the salon co-owner, did my hair. When she was done, the women in the beauty parlor all said it was a fantastic new look. Rachel called it a choppy crop with baby bangs. Whatever it was, it was the perfect arrangement for me with my black hair. One woman said that with my green eyes, I looked like a movie star. When I saw myself in the mirror, it was like seeing a new person. Still, I couldn't let myself be pleased, not after what I'd learned about Jess and what I suspected Bridget had learned about Bleeder.

From the beauty shop I went straight to the hospital to see Jess. When she and I spotted each other, we started screaming like we used to do. She was in a semiprivate room, lying flat on her back with all sorts of tubes jutting out of various parts of her body. Luckily, there was no one else in the room besides Jess to overhear our outburst.

"Ida Mae, you look fabulous. I love your hair."

"Thanks. There's so much to tell you, Jess. I don't know where to start."

"Ida Mae, I heard about the wedding."

"It was very hectic, what with Bleeder's orders and all. Otherwise, you'd have been there."

"My absence made your Momma happy, I'm sure, considering how much she always hated me."

"She doesn't hate you, Jess, but I admit she was a pain in the ass toward you. When I called her to tell her about your condition, Momma started to cry. Right on the phone. She said to give you her best. She wants to come and see you."

"Oh, that'll be interesting." Jess paused. "I hear that you're a singer now."

"Yeah, in a manner of speaking. But I do love it. I got a music scholarship to Pitt, but I'm scared to death about going."

"That's wonderful news, Ida Mae. You'll do just fine."

We talked for an hour or more. Before the disease, Jess was every bit as beautiful as her mother, with identical jet-black hair and piercing black eyes. Now pale and drawn, she had lost that beauty as well as most of her hair. Her skin was wrinkled and pale, as if she'd been held under water too long.

We both heard the knock at the door.

Momma entered.

"Oh, you poor child," Momma cried. "What's happened to you?"

"Wish I knew, Mrs. Glockley. It's some new thing I picked up from a toilet seat."

Nobody laughed at Jess's attempt at humor.

Momma continued, "And chile, I don't want you to call me Mrs. Glockley anymore. I'm Penny—always was, always will be."

Jess was crying now, and so was Momma.

Momma continued, "Jess, I'm sorry I treated you so badly."

"It's okay, Penny. I'm white trash, and I'm getting just what I deserve. It's a punishment from God."

"Nonsense, chile. God is forgiving and loving and full of goodness. He doesn't zap people. Instead, He's always ready to love us, always. You were just a child when you did those things, and you're still a child. God is no child molester, no sir. That disease was in your genes, that's all."

"They tell me that I'm going to die. I'm only nineteen years old—nineteen! I haven't lived. I haven't married. I haven't seen anything. If God's so great, then let Him get me out of this."

She was crying openly.

"Miracles are few and far between, chile," Momma said. "You can't count on getting one. If God got all of us out of our troubles every time we got into it, life wouldn't have any meaning."

"You sound like my mother now," Jess said. "Bridget has studied my lifeline, what little there is of it, and she's read my fortune in the cards. She doesn't offer much hope, either, but she's convinced that God played no part in it."

I was listening to the conversation between them, not saying a word. Then Momma placed a hand on Jess's head.

"Chile, I love you and God loves you. I'm so sorry for my conduct in the past. Please forgive me."

"Of course, I forgive you."

Well, I had to get out of there without delay before I burst into sobs. I was very proud of Momma. At that moment, I loved her very much. She stayed after I departed but left shortly afterwards.

I came back to see Jess four more times before she died. At the memorial service, Bridget could not stop crying. She wore oversized sunglasses to hide her eyes and, of course, a black outfit. As the casket was being lowered, she pitched forward onto the muddy ground until a bystander nearby helped her up.

Having lost her only daughter, she was depressed for several months afterwards. During that time, Momma and Bridget became close friends.

Chapter 6

By late summer, I was off to school in the big city. Having a roommate helped eliminate my homesickness and my grief. Connie Charles was a Highland Park girl from Pittsburgh's East End. On several weekends, she took me home with her. The meal was always perfect, and her parents treated me like one of the family. In one dinner discussion, Connie's father pointed out that nightlife on Walnut Street in the Oakland section of the city was thriving, prompting me to find a spot there that featured bluegrass. After Dodger agreed to make the commute, we got a gig. He'd travel back and forth between Pittsburgh and Mammoth Falls, staying in a cheap motel when he visited the city, frequently with other band members from West Virginia.

Meanwhile, I became a dual major—music and English—and signed up for a creative writing class, which required a trip to the Cathedral of Learning building three times a week. On the elevator to attend class on the first day, I encountered many fellow students who were as harassed and befuddled as I was, even the older students headed for law school on one of the top floors.

Being a small-town girl, I considered the Cathedral to be the size of a skyscraper, a viewpoint that mellowed somewhat when

I learned its actual height. Even so, it stood spikelike in sharp contrast to the other structures in the Oakland area, and from my classroom on the fifth floor, it offered a panoramic view of the campus.

Professor Jenkins helped with my spelling and grammar and my classroom presentations. In due course, my bad grammar disappeared plus a good portion of my accent. To my surprise, I also discovered that I had a writing talent, at least according to Professor Jenkins. In the meantime, the success of our small band at a bar called Smokies on Walnut Street became well known. Dodger assured me that my tight jeans and sultry singing voice were the primary reasons that the male audience kept increasing.

"Ida Mae, I can't even estimate the number of guys who've asked me about you. When I tell them you're happily married, their faces drop and they slink away. I don't think you realize how attractive you are."

"Dodger, you're too kind."

Smokies was aptly named. By midnight, you could hardly see your hand in front of your face thanks to the buildup of cigar and cigarette smoke. My eyes were always burning and bloodshot by the time I got back to the dorm.

Letters from Bleeder kept coming, but he couldn't say where he was or what he did. Reading between the lines, I could tell that he was scared stiff. We wrote to each other almost daily, and when his letters stopped coming, I got extremely anxious. Still, I couldn't let myself think that something bad had happened to him.

One day, Connie announced to me that a soldier in uniform was waiting in the dorm lobby with a message for me. Right then, I knew that Bleeder had been killed and concluded that if I could avoid going downstairs, I could keep Bleeder alive that much longer. It was Connie who finally persuaded me to meet with the soldier.

"Are you Ida Mae Glockley Thompson, wife of Roy Thompson?" the soldier asked.

"Yes."

My throat and mouth were so dry I could barely speak. It was like talking through cotton.

"I regret to inform you that your husband has been killed in action. He died a brave soldier who came to the aid of his fallen comrades. His body is being shipped back home. You'll receive additional details very soon."

"Thank you." My words were barely audible.

"I'm terribly sorry," the soldier said.

Then he was gone, having given me some papers that I couldn't read. The pain was intense. By the time I opened the door to my room, I was sobbing uncontrollably. For the next two days, I couldn't leave the room and when I finally emerged, it seemed the entire campus was aware of my plight. People were constantly expressing sympathy, including professors I didn't even know. I had always heard that Pittsburgh was the warmest, friendliest city on earth, but I had no idea that its universities followed that same tradition.

When I returned to Mammoth Falls for Bleeder's funeral, the entire village seemed to have shrunk. That was understandable considering that I'd been in the big city for so long. Even structures I once considered mammoth seemed tiny. That weekend, Connie and I stayed with my parents. It seemed to me that the entire valley had turned out. Reverend Highwater was magnificent, as usual.

When I first saw the flag-draped coffin, I almost lost it. Then later, when one of the officers handed me the flag at the gravesite, neatly folded, I really did lose it. Still crying, I spoke to Bleeder under my breath. "Goodbye, Bleeder. I will miss you, big time."

I know he heard me.

I realized then that I could never return on a permanent basis and that I'd never again see Mammoth Falls the same. Pittsburgh was now my home. Bleeder's funeral was particularly sad because I knew that in addition to him, I was expressing my goodbyes to my family, to Mammoth Falls, and to Bridget all at once.

At one point at the cemetery, I noticed a young man of color trying to make eye contact with me. Sporting an Afro, he was very young, probably in his early twenties. When the service was over, he approached me.

"Mrs. Thompson, let me express my sympathies. I was in Vietnam with your husband."

"You knew Bleeder?" I asked.

"Yes, I knew him very well. I fought with him, and I was with him when he died."

He told me that his name was Evan Kress. I told him I couldn't talk to him at any length because of the number of mourners vying for my attention. I suggested that he call me Ida Mae and told him that I wanted to spend additional time with him later to learn more about Bleeder. At that point, he suggested that we ride back together if I had room, adding that he had been planning to go back on the bus.

"We have plenty of room," I said.

In the car later, Evan began the conversation by telling us he'd gotten a job in Pittsburgh with Heinz. "I'll be joining the training program. My plan is to become a salesman while getting an MBA at night."

Riding in the passenger seat beside Connie, who had borrowed her father's car for the trip, I turned toward the backseat to direct my next inquiry. "Tell me about Bleeder."

"Bleeder should never have been over there. He was too sensitive, too accident-prone. Even after we learned to fire M-16s, there was a real question in my mind, and in his, whether he would be able to kill anyone. He was like a fish out of water."

"Go on."

"Bleeder would do anything for you if he considered you a

friend, and his friendship was a godsend to me. It's not easy being a Black man in the armed services, let me tell you. Bleeder was always there, ready to support me if someone got out of line. He may have been an improbable soldier, but he was a wonderful friend. Everyone seemed to like him. During basic, he led a prayer group in our barracks."

"Sounds like Bleeder."

"It wasn't all flowers and roses for Bleeder, though. The sergeant in charge of our squad badgered him unmercifully."

"Why was that?" Connie asked, joining the conversation.

"Vietnam was a peculiar war. The gooks would come at you during the night and then disappear during the day. We knew damn well where they were hiding. If they didn't go underground to use the tunnels, they would disappear into the various villages and hamlets that dotted the landscape. It wasn't that hard to figure that out." He paused. "In most cases, we returned to base at night. On one patrol, however, we slept out in our bags for three nights in a row. In the field over there it was impossible to sleep for long. What with the mushy ground and the heat and the bugs and the fear of night attacks, you were lucky to get fifteen minutes. So . . . on this night we were tired and cranky and our sergeant—we called him Thunder Balls—who on a normal day was mean as a weasel was on the warpath."

He paused again.

"Well, anyway, late in the afternoon, one of our men got popped by a sniper—hit in the head. That set us off, let me tell you. In a fury, we searched for the sniper—without success—but we did find a little village close by. The sergeant wanted vengeance. His conclusion was that the sniper had come out of that village."

"I can sense what's coming," Connie said.

"It wasn't pretty, let me tell you. One of the soldiers in our squad spoke Vietnamese. Through him we told the mayor of this hamlet that he had fifteen minutes to produce the culprit, failing which we would shoot three hostages. The mayor denied they were hiding anyone, but Thunder Balls didn't believe him and he had already picked out three hostages—two men, one a young man in his twenties, the other much older—and a woman in her fifties."

"Was he bluffing?" Connie asked.

"The sergeant wasn't one to bluff. When the fifteen minutes were up, they would die, he said, unless the mayor produced the sniper."

"What happened?" I asked.

"When the time limit expired, the lieutenant turned to Bleeder and demanded that he pop the three hostages. Don't get me wrong. His choice of Bleeder wasn't a fluke. He'd been badgering him unmercifully for weeks."

"What did Bleeder do?" Connie asked.

"Bleeder flat-out refused to shoot them, saying it was against military and moral law; whereupon the sergeant drew his pistol and dispatched all three with three quick blasts."

"How awful," Connie said.

"Right, but it was happening every day, all the time. It was easy for the sergeant to do the killing. He was a homicidal maniac. But it was something else for a man like Bleeder, sweet as he was, to kill three innocent people."

"Is that what caused the rift between Bleeder and the officer?" Connie asked.

"Not exactly. There was bad blood between them even prior to this incident. But on that occasion, in the sergeant's mind, Bleeder had disobeyed a direct order. Didn't matter none that the order involved the killing of innocent civilians."

"What happened next?" I asked.

"After we got back to the base, from that point forward, Bleeder got every shit job that the sergeant could dish out. If there was a latrine to dig, Bleeder dug it. If there was a particularly nasty patrol coming up, Bleeder always got picked for it. We watched and wondered how long Bleeder would be able to survive."

"Poor Bleeder," I said.

"Yes, and one day Bleeder and the sergeant, they went out together on what the sergeant said was a 'special patrol.' Thunder Balls came back carrying Bleeder over his shoulder—"

"Was he . . . " I couldn't bring myself to verbalize the obvious question.

"Oh, he was dead, alright. The only trouble was, the wound was in his back. If Thunder Balls was standing directly behind him when the shot was fired, that would be extremely important for obvious reasons."

"You don't suggest that—"

"I didn't know what to think. I only knew that they hated each other. The two of them went out on patrol and only one came back . . . alive. You figure it."

"What's the sergeant's real name?" I asked.

"Leonid Ratchnik."

"Polish?" I asked.

"Probably Russian," he answered.

"Won't they punish him?" Connie asked.

"No way. Nobody said a word. Besides, he's the type of brute they want in command."

"How did you get out of there?" Connie asked.

"My tour of duty was up two days after Bleeder died."

When we arrived in Pittsburgh, I thanked Evan for his openness and wished him luck at Heinz. A short time after I returned, I got word that Daddy had died. Despite not talking much, he was a good man who loved his family and his country dearly. Without warning, a stroke had killed him. Momma seemed to be handling things well enough, but she was good at hiding her true feelings. We both knew that a stroke was a good way to go. As it turned out, Connie was out of town, so I was forced to take public transportation to the funeral. When Momma picked me up at the bus station, she wasn't crying.

"Seems all we do is bring you down here for funerals," she said.

"How're you doing, Momma?"

"Better than I expected."

"He was a good man."

And then we both said it at the same time: "BUT HE DIDN'T TALK MUCH."

We both laughed.

"It was a good marriage," she said. "I enjoyed his company, and he enjoyed mine. There was love, a deep love. He didn't go to church much, but he was religious all the same. I'm sure God will have mercy on his soul."

"I'm sure He will, Momma."

I hadn't called her that in awhile. She looked over at me and smiled.

The memorial service was conducted in our home. When I looked in the casket, it was as though they had substituted a stranger. The man didn't look like my father at all. Even his hair was a different color. I was sure it was someone else, but I pretended not to notice. Then, when we got to the gravesite and I saw the headstone with my father's name on it, I thought I'd better say something.

"Momma, it's not Daddy. They're burying a stranger."

"Nonsense, dear. It's your father all right. It's just a bad fix. He never wore lipstick in his life."

"Momma, the dyed hair wasn't right. We've buried a transvestite!"

"Relax, dear. I checked for the tattoo he put on his arm right after we were married, and it was there."

"Daddy had a tattoo?"

My conversation with Reverend Highwater in his office that same day was compelling.

"Ida Mae, I'm so sorry about your father. He was a good man, a gentle man. He didn't come to church that often, but I know he was God-fearing. And I'm so sorry about Bleeder."

"Thank you, Pastor. Momma and I will miss them both very much."

"What can I do for you, Ida Mae?"

"While I'm down here, I'd like to clarify a few things. I don't suppose there's any biblical restriction against having sex once you're a widow?"

"That isn't correct, Ida Mae. Any sex outside of marriage is forbidden."

"You mean if I don't choose to remarry right away, which I won't, I've got to wait until I do?"

"I'm afraid that's correct?"

"Pastor, that's ridiculous. One of the Commandments speaks in terms of *adultery*, a prohibition of sex outside of marriage. That makes sense for a person who's married, but I'm not married. I'm a widow. Also, I can understand why someone contemplating marriage for the first time might choose to remain chaste.'

He nodded.

I continued, "So long as a person remains clueless as to what intercourse is like, it's not altogether unreasonable to ask that person to wait. But I've experienced it. I know how great it is. Pastor, I've tried it, and I like it—a lot. And I've got no immediate plans to remarry. That being the case, there's no way in the world that I'll be able to resist indefinitely. It's as simple as that."

"Ida Mae, for all you know you could be remarried tomorrow. Then, you'll have the protection of your marriage vows."

"Look, Reverend, I loved my husband very much. Out of respect for him, I won't even think about getting remarried for at least five years, maybe more. Even so, the first stirrings of my sexual desire are already present."

"Ida Mae, you mustn't act on them. It would be sinful."

"Who made up these silly rules anyway?"

"It's what the Good Book tells us."

"Pastor, I know that Jesus, the Lamb of God, perfect in every way, was sacrificed for the benefit of mankind. Since he was perfect, obviously he didn't experience sex with anyone while he was here on earth."

"That's true," he said.

"That's where the problem lies, Pastor. Without knowing the driving effects of passion on a person who has previously experienced sex in marriage, how could Jesus have endorsed those rules?"

"You think there should be no restrictions at all?"

"I think there should be limited restrictions. Absolution should come for people who've been exposed to sex through marriage, at least once, and who don't expect to get remarried immediately, if at all."

"Well, it all seems very logical, I must say. Still, you're at odds with Scripture."

"No, Reverend. The Scripture is at odds with me."

We laughed together.

Chapter 7

From the moment I returned to the university, I began to feel like something was missing. Looking back on it, I suppose I was still in my grieving period caused by Bleeder's death combined with Daddy's passing. I tried to get back to a normal routine but just couldn't pull it off. School was no longer interesting to me. And the thrill I used to experience singing with the band on Walnut Street had also disappeared. I needed something more, and I wasn't sure just what that was.

More and more I thought about Bleeder. Here was a man who'd given his life to fight in a far-off war, a poor boy from West Virginia who tried to do the right thing and died in the process, while I remained comfortably stateside. Even if the war was unjust and immoral, it was not unjust or immoral because of anything Bleeder did. Most of all, I wondered about the circumstances surrounding his death.

I suppose the demonstrations here at home really tipped the balance for me. I began to feel sorry for innocent soldiers like Evan, who had survived only to get hit with the backlash. These men had done nothing wrong aside from serving their country in a time of crisis, a sacrifice that brought them nothing when they returned stateside. It was ironic. It wasn't that I was becoming less negative about the war itself. Instead, my sympathies toward the men who had to fight there was growing much stronger.

All I knew was that I could no longer sit idly by while young men were giving their all for a cause that would only bring them infamy and disgrace. So at nineteen years old, I joined the Women's Army Corps. Momma and Connie were beside themselves when I told them.

"You can't do it, Ida Mae. You'll get yourself killed," Connie said in our room.

"If I do, I do. But I've got to go."

Momma was just as vocal over the phone. "Are you out of your fucking mind?"

I'd never heard her use that word.

Not long after basic training, I landed at Tan Son Nhut Air Base outside of Saigon. I arrived as a private first class, thirsting to make a difference in a war that was going nowhere.

Our descent into the airport involved a steep dive, presumably because of ground fire, that made me hold on for dear life to keep from being thrown forward. Once landed, a group of soldiers with heavy weapons escorted us into a yellow school bus.

"Say, driver, what's the chicken wire over the windows for?" I asked.

"It's to repel any hand grenades the gooks try to throw in."

"Oh, that's comforting," I said.

My orders said I'd be stationed permanently at the air base. I wrote to Momma, Connie, and Bridget regularly, but I never fully described the horrors that we were facing daily. Those atrocities paled considerably when compared to the bloodbath occurring in the countryside. Constantly, I would hear about men brought in without limbs, without sight or burned by napalm. Nor did I write to them about the rocket attacks that occurred nightly. Instead, I wrote about Lieutenant Happy Olson, who showed up in a reserve shelter during a rocket attack. He rolled in a few minutes behind me.

"Nothing like a night attack to increase the range of one's acquaintances," he said.

I laughed.

"Tell me your name," he said.

"I'm Ida Mae Glockley." I'd begun to use my maiden name.

"With a name like that, you can only be from West Virginia."

"Right you are."

"The faint accent helped a little. Let me introduce myself. I'm Hap Olson."

"Nice to meet you, Mr. Hap Olson."

"You don't really use the name *Ida Mae* do you?"

"Well, my husband, before he died, God rest his soul, used to call me Puggy on occasion."

"A good choice. I'll call you Puggy. What happened to your husband?"

"Killed in action—right here in Nam."

"Is that why you're here?"

"Partly. How about you?"

"I volunteered for duty with the Marine Corps right after law school. A lot of the guys got out of the draft by getting their wives pregnant in the last year. I never got around to marriage, so I missed that opportunity."

"Too bad."

He smiled back at me.

We started dating right after that. Hap was not exactly handsome. Still, he had a dignity about him because of his height (six feet, at least) that made him very attractive and sexy. When he smiled, the angels sang, and when he called me Puggy, I would melt. WHOOOEEE!

Our romance grew quickly. Thankfully, his duty did not require him to go on patrol. "Paper shuffler" was the term he used. My job wasn't any more challenging than his, so we both had ample time to see each other. Eventually, we took a seven-day leave together to Hawaii. Unclothed, he looked strong and powerful, but his kindness and gentleness came through just the same. When we made love, he was tender and loving.

Apparently, that same gentleness and dignity was evident to others. Everyone seemed to adore him. While sightseeing at Pearl Harbor, he was stunned by what he saw.

"The Japs really did a job on us," he said.

We were standing at the shoreline looking at the capsized *Arizona*.

"Yes," I answered.

"I've got a theory about that," he said.

"About what?"

"Pearl Harbor . . . the attack, I mean."

"Let's hear it."

We stood together at the memorial holding hands. It was a bright, sunny day. The sounds from the harbor never ceased, mostly associated with various small craft that gave off a rattling sound.

"FDR wanted us to be in that war in the worst way," he said.

"Why would he want that?"

"Simple . . . the Brits were hanging by a thread. Hitler was in France. England would be next. After that, maybe Canada, then us. We couldn't afford to wait, and he knew it." He smiled at me. "Even so, it wouldn't be easy, considering the vast amount of antiwar sentiment that existed in the country. He had to come in through the back door, so to speak. He had to provoke the Japanese in the Pacific, but he had to move cautiously. There had to be an incident severe enough to result in a declaration of war."

"You mean that FDR enticed the Japanese to attack us?"

"Sure. It was the only way to get us into the war."

"I don't see how that follows."

"Japan, Italy, and Germany had signed a tripartite agreement whereby a declaration of war against any one of them would involve the others."

"I see."

"He knew there'd be a negative reaction to the embargoes he was imposing against Japan, but he was gambling on the fact that any reprisals would come in the Philippines or some other such location but never Pearl Harbor. It was too far from the mainland."

"I'm getting the picture."

"Because his assumption was wrong, his gamble didn't pay off and some three thousand service men stationed here lost their lives because of it."

I nodded.

"You can't make an omelet without cracking a few eggs," he said.

"You can't be serious," I sputtered.

"I'm damn serious."

The conversation ended at that moment. We stood silently observing the capsized battleship. Hap said that hundreds of sailors were entombed there. Standing where we were, I thought of them, trapped below, dead all these years.

"I'm not saying that FDR knew the day or the hour or the location. I am saying that he provoked the Japs with embargoes and submarines in Japanese waters and by placing the fleet at Pearl Harbor. He made the raid a foregone conclusion, although none of the Army or Navy brass picked up on it."

"Thank God we entered the war when we did. Otherwise, we might be speaking German," I said.

"Or Japanese," he added. "And it all worked like clockwork. The US declared war on Japan thereby provoking Germany to declare war on us some four days later."

"And it became a popular war, unlike the one we're fighting now," I said.

Our hotel in Hawaii had a reputation for serving good food, so we decided to try it. At dinner that night, Hap wore white pants, a Hawaiian shirt with blue and pink flowers, and sandals. I was wearing a casual dress in the same shade of blue and white sandals. In front of us on the table sat a large glass bowl containing a floating white gardenia.

"Puggy, that's what I call a wonderful centerpiece. Can you smell it?"

"An aroma from the gods," I added and abruptly changed the subject. "Hap, if I wanted to track down a particular soldier, how would I do it?" I asked casually.

"What branch?"

"Army."

"In my job, I've had to track down many servicemen. It's a matter of going to Saigon. The records are kept there."

I told him Bleeder's story.

"And so, you want to learn all you can about this Ratchnik fellow," he said.

"Yes."

"Tell you what, the next time I go to Saigon, I'll check the records for you. Better yet, I'll bring you along."

That night, we were barely through the door to our room when we were kissing wildly and removing clothes. Afterwards, on the bed he propped himself up on one elbow.

"You have the most incredible body I've ever seen."

"Yours isn't so bad either," I answered.

What I appreciated most about Hap—aside from his body—was his sense of humor. He was constantly seeing the comedy in situations that seemed highly frustrating to me. The unidentified meat on Tuesdays at the base became "mystery meat." The almost-nightly rocket attacks from the Viet Cong became "unwanted mail."

We adored each other, and it wasn't long before we were talking about marriage, which Hap described as "pitching forward," presumably a term he chose because of his anxious anticipation. Naturally, we elected to wait until we got back to the States.

Hap admitted that he had not had wonderful success with women. When he was a teenager, he said, his idea of an orgy was to buy multiple sex magazines. Because I couldn't find a flaw in him, I began to feel that he was too good for me. His family had an estate on the Main Line in Philadelphia. How would they react to their only son marrying a plain nobody from Mammoth Falls, West Virginia? Despite his assurances that all would go well, I became more and more discouraged. I would pick fights with him for no reason just to feel the assurances that came when we made up.

Momma told me in her letters that I was being ridiculous, as did Connie. Bridget went even further. She warned me that the war made everything uncertain and that I should treat any time with Hap as a gift. I suppose Bridget's letter was what turned me around. Shortly after it arrived, Hap and I met at our usual location.

"Hap, I'm sorry I've been such a pain. I'll try to do better in the future."

"Puggy, you're everything to me, you know that. We're going to be married, and we're going to live together happily after that, end of story."

"I just hope you know what you're getting into, that's all. I'm beer. You're champagne. You're from the Main Line. I'm from the end of the line."

"Please quit being negative. You're the classiest lady I know.

What's more, I love you madly, passionately. All is well, and it will ever be."

Eventually, Hap got the Saigon assignment he'd anticipated. It was an opportunity for me to check military records. When he picked me up in the borrowed Jeep, I winced when I saw the M-16 on the seat behind us.

"I assume it's loaded," I said.

"Correct."

"I also assume you know how to use it," I said.

"Correct again."

"Are we going to drive the entire way?"

"No . . . too dangerous. This vehicle will get us to the airport. I've arranged for us to jump an air transport."

When we left the car, he put his firearm in the trunk. By and by, we came to the Army's document registry. We were both admitted under Hap's special pass. In short order, we located the appropriate files. Ratchnik's card was right where it was supposed to be.

"He's dead," Hap said.

"How do you know?"

"Do you see that designation in the upper right-hand corner—*KIA*? That means killed in action."

I found myself frustrated and angry, knowing that I would never find out what really happened on that patrol. On the other hand, I was relieved to know that Ratchnik wasn't enjoying life at Bleeder's expense.

I wanted so much for my relationship with Hap to be perfect, but relationships are never perfect. Bridget kept pointing this out in her letters. We had such a wonderful time together, experienced so much fun together, that in time I came to agree with Hap's positive assessment of our chances. *Our marriage will work out well*, I thought. How glorious was the complete love we felt between us.

Then one night it happened.

The rockets came out of nowhere and made a direct hit on Hap's quarters. It was the first attack of the evening, unexpected and sudden. There was no way to prepare for it, no time to get to the shelter. Hap was killed instantly.

I cried for three days straight.

Chapter 8

"He's a sick fuck," the soldier next to me said.

I did not reply. I was standing a short distance from the Tan Son Nhut mortuary, where bodies were prepared for shipment overseas. I was here to pick up Hap's personal effects, to ship them to his family.

I looked at the man who had addressed me. The soldier's name tag told me that I'd been singled out by a man named Fleming. He appeared to be referring to a soldier some distance away who was lining up aluminum caskets for the trip home. When I didn't answer, he continued, "You probably wonder why I think he's a sick fuck."

I kept quiet.

"Well, I'll tell you why."

He tossed away his cigarette butt, spat once, and proceeded to tell me. "This is a horrible place to work. Do you notice the smell?"

I nodded.

"Krakow and I receive the incoming KIAs. Most often, they arrive in body bags. We identify them, tag them, and transfer them to the mortuary so that the bodies can be prepared for shipment home. It takes at least a day to get them ready. Then, we put the finished product into aluminum caskets. Next, we line up the caskets in the yard over there. Last, we supervise the loading of the caskets into transports—like that one over there—for shipment overseas. The difference between Krakow and me is that he's on his third hitch over here. He loves this work. He treats dead bodies as though they were his children."

He paused to spit.

"He's a sick fuck, I tell you. I go crazy dealing with the KIAs—husbands, sons, brothers, fathers, uncles—all with their hopes and dreams shattered; all with their lives ended. I can't tell you how many caskets I've handled since I was assigned here, each one shiny and silver colored, or the number of body bags we put inside, all made of green plastic, always the same color, with white nylon stripes."

"It sounds like a tough job," I said.

"It's horrible. I've got to get out of here before I go nuts."

Another soldier came over, an African American I estimated to be in his twenties. The name tag identified him as Jones. He obviously had overheard our conversation.

"Anyone who stays here a minute longer than he has to is crazy, man," Jones said. "This place is pure hell—hell on earth. You see those caskets neatly lined up over there—"

He pointed. I nodded.

"Well, three of them carry men from my company. They were killed in a Viet Cong ambush. I'm here delivering their personal effects. The lieutenant asked me to make sure their stuff went with them. People steal stuff out of those body bags."

Jones paused. Fleming was listening intently.

Pointing to the caskets, Jones said, "It's awfully quiet now, but you should've seen what was happening to those poor bastards during the attack. You know how it works, don't you?"

I tried to respond. "Well, I—"

"We're guinea pigs, man. We're out there on patrol to draw

fire, pure and simple. On this particular day, three brothers—we called them Huey, Dewey, and Louie—were out front. Without warning, man, all hell broke loose. There was a burst of fire from automatic weapons. Huey went down. He was severely wounded and screaming. Meanwhile, additional automatic weapons opened up. We were surrounded."

He stopped to look directly into my eyes.

"Do you know what the lieutenant did?" Jones asked.

I shook my head.

"He called in a napalm strike—without worrying about his own men. Dewey and Louie were both caught in it. Do you know what a body looks like when it's burned enough to cause death?"

"It's not pretty," Fleming said.

"No, it's not, especially when you have to listen to the screams before they die. These are poor kids, all Black, my brothers, each from the ghetto of an American city. Not one of them was older than twenty-two. Man, these are the people who are fighting this war."

"Say, the man who ordered the strike," I said, "his name wasn't Ratchnik was it?"

"No . . . Shaeffer. Why do you ask?"

"I knew a soldier named Ratchnik, that's all."

By this time, Krakow had been attracted to our gathering. "What did you say, Fleming?" he said.

"Krakow, I was just telling these people that you're a sick fuck because you like this job," Fleming said.

Krakow's eyes widened. "If you believe that, you're crazier than I thought. This job sucks, and you know it."

"You're on your third hitch," Fleming said.

"I can explain that" he said with a smile. "I dislike my wife more than I dislike this war."

We all laughed.

Chapter 9

Just as soon as I was able to do so gracefully, I resigned so that I could return to the States. On my return, I elected to visit San Francisco, which I'd never visited but had heard wonderful things about. Soon, I found a place to stay there. As it turned out, Connie's cousin Stella Freeze had been looking for a roommate. When she greeted me at the door, I was struck by her height, at least six feet, accentuated by a long pink robe that hung down to her bunny slippers still in place at two in the afternoon. Her apartment was neat as a pin, but her appearance belied all that—shaggy brown hair that sprouted everywhere in a curly mass despite the Indian headband that branded her in my mind as a consummate hippie.

In a deep voice she offered coffee, which I declined, and explained that she had been working on her novel, obviously in longhand judging from the pile of papers on a nearby desk. The room was smoke-filled as was confirmed by the pile of butts in a pan lid that served as an ashtray and by the cigarette that dangled from her mouth. Black horn-rimmed glasses contrasted sharply with her ash-white skin. I dropped my gear in a corner and asked her if she wanted to join me for a walk to acquaint me with her city. She declined but gave suggestions about possible areas of interest.

On my walk, an Episcopalian church enticed me to enter despite how much of a pure-bred Presbyterian I was. The singing that emanated from the sanctuary as I passed by and my fondness for uplifting Episcopalian pageantry had lured me in. The church was packed. An usher took me down the center aisle. When I gestured that I would like to sit in an open spot in the second row, he told me, very nicely, that that particular area was reserved for the rector's family. Acceding to his wishes, I sat one row behind.

The church was done up in all its finery with Easter lilies evident everywhere. The pounding organ added to the mood. A few minutes later, the same usher who was so cordial to me was now escorting a woman with two small children to the row in front of me. I assumed that she was the rector's wife, an attractive woman, obviously proud of her young daughter and son. The little girl appeared to be about four, her brother a few years older, both towheaded.

Soon after they sat down, there came a clashing of cymbals and a pounding of drums as the procession began making its way slowly down the main aisle to the front of the church, with the rector in the last position, a man in his mid-thirties wearing garments of fine cloth joined by a choir and assistant ministers in the lead. I wondered what the young children would do when they saw their father coming toward them.

Standing at the outer edge of the pew closest to the aisle, the little girl and her brother were content to wave at him and smile as he passed by. To his credit, even as resplendent as he was in all his finery, the rector managed to wiggle a little finger in their direction—to their utter delight. The members of the procession got into positions at the front of the sanctuary and sat down when the hymn was completed.

I had forgotten that the Episcopalians did everything by script. Several times, the members of the congregation were halfway into the text before I had even found the appropriate page. All seemed to know what page of the prayer book was involved. Soon, the rector's assistant proceeded to the pulpit to present the homily. He was a young man, probably in his twenties. He was about ten minutes in when something happened that no one could have predicted.

"DADDY!"

It was the little girl in front of me. She had spotted her father in his seat in the chancel. Several in the congregation wondered later just what it was that set her off. To that point, she had been very good, very quiet. Perhaps it was that she had been waiting so long. Perhaps it was the experience of listening to words from someone so high up and far off, words she could not understand. Perhaps she was just tired.

Whatever the reason, the little girl felt no compunction about shouting her father's name in the middle of the homily as she ran up the chancel steps to sit on his lap. Of course, the congregation was delighted. The rector held her for a few minutes, hugging her. The congregation giggled and laughed. Her mother, obviously embarrassed, arrived to escort her back to her seat.

Thus interrupted, the assistant minister in the pulpit took a wise course.

"Need I go on?" he asked. "After all, we have just seen evidence of what the Easter story is all about."

Following one or two readings and a final hymn that was sung with renewed gusto, the service ended with a recessional back up the main aisle. When the youngsters' father passed a second time, his little finger wiggled at them again to their obvious delight. It was much more than just a cute incident. It was proof that the Bible is accurate when it directs us to learn from the little children.

Chapter 10

While I enjoyed the Episcopalian church experience, I remained a Presbyterian through and through. My religious roots were too strong to overcome. And my roommate's Presbyterian heritage meant that we could attend church together—which gave me incentive to go with her to services, and we did so, regularly.

Soon, certain members of the congregation got word that I was looking for a job. Within a week, I had my first interview, which resulted in a gig as a backup receptionist for a local law firm.

The job turned out to be a snap. I arrived at seven a.m. to cover the front desk until the regular receptionist appeared. Then, I was on again at the front desk at noon, when once again I filled in for the regular receptionist during her lunch break. When I wasn't doing her job, I sat at a secondary reception desk on the second floor. The phones were usually very quiet during the times assigned to me since most people avoided calling in the early morning or during the lunch hour. What's more, most callers used the direct dial option, thereby avoiding the receptionist altogether. The second floor was never busy. Most attorneys passed by my desk on the way to their offices without saying a word.

"Well, halloo, sweetie."

Even though I'd checked the photo album previously, I couldn't place this man. He was probably in his early sixties, and, if so, the years hadn't been kind to him as was evident from his wrinkles. His crow's feet were pronounced, but that was not the least of it. Extra skin under his chin flapped when he spoke. It looked like the comb on a rooster held upside down.

"Aren't you a beauty? I hope you're not married," he said.

"Thank you. I'm a widow."

"How fortunate for me. What do they call you?"

I told him my name.

"You're kidding. A person with a name like that has to be right off the farm." He laughed.

I elected not to respond.

"Well, my name is Davit Nesbitt."

I gave him a blank stare.

"I'm head of the estate section," he said.

"Good morning, Mr. Nesbitt," I said.

"Good morning to you."

My telephone began ringing, and he left for his office. Later, I found myself sharing the lunchroom with one of the secretaries.

"I'm Trudy," she said. "I understand that you're the new receptionist."

"Backup receptionist." I smiled and told her my name.

"You're very attractive," Trudy said. "Just what we need out there. Let's see, you've been here one day. Undoubtedly, Nesbitt has already hit on you."

"As a matter of fact—"

We both laughed.

"What's his problem?" I asked.

"It's called being an asshole," Trudy said.

We laughed again.

"He's married, but that doesn't stop him. He considers

himself to be God's gift to women."

"You don't mean it. He's so puny, old, and pasty."

"Yes, but he's also a powerful member of the firm, and some women here are attracted to that, mostly secretaries, usually the ugly ones."

"Thank you for being so open with me."

"In this crazy place, be very careful what you say and where you say it. There are rats and snitches everywhere. If there is anyone else in the lunchroom, I'll clam up on you. Let me warn you now."

Trudy told me that she ate in the lunchroom at the same time every day and I probably would see her there again. She worked for Brenda Foltz, "a real saint," according to Trudy.

"If Nesbitt or any other lawyer gives you a hard time, let me know. I'll take you to see Brenda. She could be a big help," Trudy said.

The next morning when I arrived, a man was sitting in the waiting room in one of the leather chairs.

"My name is Tom Lieberman," he said. "Do you know why cannibals don't eat clowns?"

"No, I don't." I smiled.

"Because they taste funny."

Corny as the joke was, I found myself laughing.

"Do you know what the three biggest Jewish holidays are?" he asked.

"Let's see—Rosh Hashanah, Hanukkah, and—"

"The Academy Awards," he said.

We laughed hard.

"I should know. I'm Jewish as hell," he said.

"Who are you here to see?" I asked.

"Ed Lieberman. He's my brother. Every time I prepare a new routine, I come in so he can hear it."

"A new routine?"

"Yes, I'm a stand-up comedian."

He explained that the automobile traffic on the way in had been much lighter than he'd anticipated, which made him about a half an hour early for his appointment. I told him where the coffee was, and a minute later, he returned with a cup.

"You need an appointment to see your brother?"

"Yeah, he's so damn busy these days that we've got to carve out a half an hour or I'll wait out here forever." He paused. "I've got another one for you. A new fellow shows up at the pool of one of the big hotels in Florida. A Jewish divorcee up in years strikes up a conversation with him. 'Tell me about yourself,' she says. He responds, 'I just got out of jail for murdering my wife.' 'Does that mean you're single?' she asks."

We laughed again.

Tom Lieberman wore a brown suit, a blue shirt, a yellow bowtie, and hiking boots. His dark wavy hair was thinning on top, an indication that his youthful appearance might be a deception. However, he'd not yet gotten the telltale paunch in the abdomen or the neck flap that would dispel all youthful estimates.

"My brother was the smart one—Cornell, Harvard Law School. I was always the cutup, the life of the party. How old would you say I am?"

"That'd be very difficult to say. You look so young."

"Thank you. I'm forty-one. My brother is four years older. He's making a ton of money here. Plus, he's got a wonderful wife and three kids. He's definitely the pick of the litter, except for my sister, who's a brain surgeon."

"She's really a brain surgeon?"

"You bet she is. Smart as hell . . . Wellesley, then Duke Medical School."

"So, there are two top picks in a litter of three." I laughed.

He drummed the fingers of his right hand on his left knee, then continued, "What do they call you, and where are you from?"

I told him.

"What did you do before coming here?"

I told him.

"Now, that takes a lot of courage. Giving up a college scholarship to become a Vietnam vet in this day and age shows real guts. Say, if I were to ask you out, I wouldn't be hitting on you. There'd be nothing to worry about."

"Oh?"

"I'm gay. I came out five years ago, which is a reason why my mother isn't speaking to me. But while you're in San Francisco you ought to see how the other half (make that the other two-thirds) lives. The Annual Ball Buster's Gala will be on Saturday. It would be tragic if you didn't get to see it. Would you like to go with me?"

"Why not?"

My roommate, Stella, had a fit when I told her. She explained that it was an annual extravaganza for cross-dressers and gays that took place at one of the local hotels. She said that during the evening all participants got screaming drunk while taking off what little clothing they had on when they showed up.

Hearing all this aroused my sense of adventure.

My first task: Put together an outfit. I chose a black full-length affair with a slit up the side, which I highlighted by wearing black fingernail polish, dark eyeshadow, and very sexy shoes all *à la* Bridget.

As I admired myself in my mirror, Stella opened our apartment door to the sight of Tom. She screamed so loud that her terror reverberated down the hallway. Tom wore a chicken costume. His orange tights looked like chicken legs, particularly with rubber feet thrown in. The chicken head featured a beak that was the same color as the feet. Yellow feathers covered his chest, lower torso, and back.

Stella's scream prompted me to rush to the living room, and

by the time I arrived, Stella and Tom were laughing hysterically. That, of course, got me to laughing too.

When things quieted down, Tom commented on my outfit. "You certainly look exotic," he said after removing his chicken head.

"I hope so," I said, smiling.

Tom drove us to the party. After we arrived, we sat briefly in the hotel lobby so he could put on his chicken feet. I asked the obvious question.

"What was your inspiration for inviting me?"

"Why did I invite you? It's very simple. You are newly arrived, so you don't know anyone. In that ballroom will be judges and clergy and professionals of all sorts. The understanding is that anything untoward that is seen or heard will be forgotten."

"Got it," I said.

Inside, it was like someone suddenly opened the doors to a lunatic asylum. Men in drag pranced around everywhere, most in high heels and many with mesh stockings. Others wore capes over leotards. Many wore lipstick, eyeshadow, and rouge in a vain attempt to imitate their female counterparts. On the other hand, many of the women did their very best to look like men, sporting trousers and mustaches and sport coats. One woman wore a tux jacket over what appeared to be black panties with black silk stockings.

Another segment favored costumes. Many birds were in evidence—ostrich, peacock, canary. Others simply wore feathers for the joy of sporting plumage—orange, red, turquoise, yellow, purple, and pink.

All the while, the music was blaring. I looked for an orchestra but saw none. Whoever was playing the tapes didn't let up for the entire evening. Tom was very nice to me. He got me drinks often and even danced with me. On the dance floor, I noticed three circular platforms overhead hanging from the ceiling that accommodated near-naked male dancers performing at that raised height.

"Would you excuse me for one minute?" I asked Tom.

On the way to the ladies' room, a person at the far end of the dance floor attracted my attention. He was in drag with feathers prominently displayed. As he was now facing in the opposite direction, he couldn't notice me until I stepped in front of him.

"Mr. Nesbitt, how are you?" I asked with a coy smile.

He turned suddenly, put his polished nails to his face, and howled. The next second, he was charging across the dance floor in heels without attempting to pick up the sequined purse that he'd dropped in the shock of seeing me.

On Monday, the head of personnel called me into his office the minute I arrived on the job. He told me that my services would no longer be required. I thought of Trudy's suggestion that I contact her boss, Brenda Foltz, if I got into trouble, but decided against it. I'd promised Tom Lieberman that I would be circumspect about the party and I intended to honor that.

Back at the apartment, I told Stella the entire story. She sympathized with me, pointing out that I was better off getting out of there.

"It's not the end of the world," she said. "Besides, you haven't seen Hollywood. That's something you must do while you're out here. As a matter of fact, I think I can get you a job there."

She explained that a good friend from college, who had opened a dress shop on Rodeo Drive a few years ago, needed an assistant.

"She offered the job to me, but I'm not ready to make the move. Her name is Holly Styles, a great lady, who makes the clothes in her shop. The last time I checked, she was making one million a year in gross sales. All the stars go there."

"It sounds fantastic," I said.

"Good. I'll tell her you're coming to see her."

Chapter 11

Holly Styles's ex-husband picked me up at the bus station. Though divorced, he and Holly continued to be partners, he told me. He did the books, handled the finances, and prepared the tax returns. She did everything else. When he told me that they had been in business for five years, he seemed proud of their success in so short a period.

"The big stars, I mean the really big ones, come to see us. And they don't seem to care in the least how much an item costs."

"That's got to be a great opportunity for you both," I said.

"You bet."

I asked him what I should call him, and he told me "Jeff" without telling me his last name. I never did find out whether Holly's last name came from him or not. After parking in the lot behind the building, he took me in the back way.

Holly's Hat was quite an enterprise. In the main display area, several mannequins featured men's and women's clothing. Glass counters showed various selections for anyone with enough audacity to meet the prices. On the way in, I noticed that one of the blouses boasted a suggested retail price of $600. Jeff took me to Holly's office, where she was sitting behind a large desk.

"Come on in," she said, standing up. "Stella has told me all about you."

She extended a hand, and I shook it. By then, Jeff had disappeared.

"What did my idiot ex-husband tell you?"

"He said that the shop is doing very well. He told me that you and he continued to be partners, even though—"

"Partners, my ass! He's an employee. I keep him around just to be nice. I'm thinking seriously about getting rid of him."

I looked down at my shoes, saying nothing.

"Listen, I need an assistant. The last two didn't work out . . . turn around."

"What?" I asked.

"Turn around."

I followed her command.

"That won't do. That won't do at all. Stella told me about your background. My clients are a sophisticated bunch. Are you willing to take advice?"

"What do you mean?"

"Are you willing to take my suggestions about your clothing?"

"What's wrong with my clothes?"

"You have a frumpy look. We need to change that—and your hair and makeup. And I expect that we'll also have to change certain of your intellectual pursuits as well."

I could feel myself reddening. "My intellectual pursuits?"

"Oh, you're beautiful and all that. It's just that here on Rodeo Drive there is a level of sophistication you might not find anywhere else. I have ten or twenty women a week applying for a sales position. I've got to tell you that I'm very selective. In a group of two hundred there may be one or two." She paused. "You've got the potential. You've definitely got the potential. But we will be forced to do a makeover."

"I'm at your disposal," I said.

"Now that's what I wanted to hear. Please pick out five outfits—anything that strikes you as sophisticated. My point is that you can't look like a frump and work here."

I felt myself reddening again, this time from anger not embarrassment. I was wearing a black dress that I had bought on sale.

"You need to have an open mind," she said. "And one other thing, darlin'—"

"What's that?"

"How can I put this? You're from West Virginia. I suspect that you haven't read a bestseller in years. That's got to change. My customers are very well-read. If they want to discuss a particular book with you, I will expect you to be responsive."

Under my breath, I started counting.

"Is there a list of books you'd like me to read?"

"I'll give you one."

And she did.

After I'd been there about three months, Jeff asked me to lunch. We got sandwiches at a takeout. Sitting in a nearby park, we watched the pigeons intrude on our conversation.

"I know she comes on kind of strong," he said, "but she's got a good heart."

"I recognize that. She's helped me find a place at no rent, a carriage house owned by one of her friends. She's given me several outfits at no charge, one of which I'm wearing right now. And she assures me that I'll make big money if I work out."

"By now, you must know what one of those dresses costs."

"I do. Not only that, she's been working to improve the sophistication of this poor little girl from West Virginia. I bet I've read twenty books in the past three months."

"What are you reading right now?"

"*To Kill a Mockingbird* by Harper Lee."

"A good choice. Just don't let her get you down. Holly can be intrusive, but she means well."

For a moment or two, we watched the pigeons.

"You still love her, don't you?"

"Is it that obvious? Yes, I do . . . very much. It was her choice to separate, not mine, and it was her idea to get the divorce. She was the one who brought us out here."

I felt very sorry for him. At one time, the two might have been equals, but over the years she'd surpassed him with her talent and intellect and, finally, her wealth. That she let him stay around was a sign of her generosity. Here was a man whose confidence had been ripped out of him, who was unable to escape a situation that could be most lethal to him. Plain looking and soft-spoken, he was the typical small-town product blinded by the lights of Hollywood.

That evening, Holly planned to drive me to my apartment while my car, a loaner she had offered me, was under repair. We hadn't taken off yet, but we were in her convertible, near the shop.

"Look! There he is," she said.

Across the street, unaware of our presence, stood a handsome beefcake of a man with brown hair. I recognized him immediately.

"His first name is Hugh, but the ladies call him Huge for obvious reasons. I discovered the accuracy of the sobriquet firsthand . . . after two or three dates," she said.

"Tell me more." I looked at her and smiled.

"Kind of like forcing an oak tree into a Dixie cup."

We both burst out laughing.

"The worst of bad fits," she said.

Even as unorthodox as she was, I liked her very much. No one would call her beautiful. Still, she had a cuteness about her that made her very attractive, a pixie look, complemented by her short brown hair and owl-brown eyes, the kind that had a bright sparkle in them evidencing an underlying friskiness. She was wearing a black power suit that gave her the look of a TV anchor. She had lunched with a high-powered Hollywood executive hours earlier.

"You see that man there." She pointed to another guy.

I nodded.

"He's a real pissant. Likes little girls—I mean little girls who are very young. I used to buy my cocaine from him until I learned about his penchant for preteens. He's sick. I won't have anything to do with him now."

"How easy is it to find a new supplier?"

"My sweet ex-husband gets it for me now. He hates to see me into blow, and he doesn't touch the stuff himself. Still, he prefers being the middleman so that he can keep an eye on me." *Blow* indeed. I was learning a new lifestyle and a new vocabulary out here that I was not particularly fond of.

Although Holly didn't claim to be an atheist, she had no church home and spent most Sunday mornings reading the Sunday paper on her balcony. Try as I might, I couldn't talk her or Jeff into joining me at the Presbyterian church Stella and I regularly attended.

By the end of the year, I had learned the business thoroughly. Several of the stars began to ask for me by name. I came to know their likes and dislikes. Holly turned out to be very generous. I was making scads of money. Consequently, I could afford tickets to most of the cultural events. I began to date three men, none seriously. What with all the expensive dinners, my waistline began to grow.

In March 1969, a thunderbolt struck us: Jeff's suicide. They found him in his apartment with half his head blown away. Close by lay a revolver, a large one. There was no note, nothing like that. Some said he did it because his health was failing. I think not. I saw it as the act of a heartbroken man rejected by the only woman he ever loved. Strangely enough, Holly was inconsolable. For the first three days, she stayed at home. When she finally did show up to work, she was still crying.

"I treated him so badly." The two of us were alone in her office. "Until his death, I didn't realize how much he meant to me. He made it clear that he frowned on my wild activities. I don't know what will become of me without his voice of moderation."

And that was the end of it. The next day she came in with dry eyes. I never again heard her mention Jeff's name.

"Listen, Ida Mae, the Academy Awards are coming up. I want you to come with me as my guest. Jeff and I have had the same seats every year, even after we divorced. The awards for this year will be held on April 14 at the Dorothy Chandler Pavilion. Bob Hope will host. Can you make it?" Holly asked.

"I'd love to go."

"Last year, because of Martin Luther King's death, the event was postponed for the first time—for forty-eight hours—so that they could put together an appropriate tribute."

"Quite a precedent," I said.

"Yes, it was."

Holly saw to it that we would be wearing evening dresses of the highest fashion, mine light blue, hers white, with all the best accessories. On the day in question, we made our way to the pavilion. We were early enough to observe Hollywood's glitterati in all its finery. When I noticed a star I could identify, I would let out a little yelp, which would invariably cause Holly to laugh.

Bob Hope provided appropriate examples of his dry wit. At one point, he referred to the awards as *Passover*, by which he was referring not to the Jewish holiday but to the number of times he had been passed over for the award.

His joke was well received. Even so, the program from that point offered little excitement.

We were in the car driving home.

"It just wasn't a good year," Holly said.

"I kept looking for Warren Beatty," I said.

"Do you have a thing for Warren?"

"Doesn't every woman?"

We laughed.

"He is adorable," she said.

Several months passed. By August, I was edgy and frustrated. I concluded that it was time to move on. I was ready to return to Mammoth Falls for a short while.

Holly and I were in her office.

"Holly, I've got to talk to you. It's not that I don't appreciate all that you've done for me. On the contrary, I'm crazy about working at the shop. It's just that I've got the jimjams, a term my father used to use."

"The *jimjams*?"

"Yes. It means you're uneasy about something and you don't know what it is, except in my case I do know the cause."

"Won't you please fill me in."

A chill settled around her words. I knew that she wasn't happy with what she knew was coming.

"It's my wanderlust," I said. "I've been dealing with it since Bleeder died. I can't stay anywhere for very long. There comes a time when I've got to move on."

"Ida Mae, I'm going to speak frankly. All those things I showered on you weren't provided totally out of friendship." She looked deep into my eyes. "I fell in love with you from the first moment I saw you."

"You mean—"

"Yes . . . love, the kind that scares most women. I didn't intend to tell you, and I wouldn't be telling you now except that I have a deep-seated fear that you're planning to leave. If there's any hope that I can stop you by telling you my true feelings, I'm going to risk it."

"You mean—"

"Oh, isn't it obvious? It can't be totally surprising to you. You're a gorgeous woman. It was these new feelings that finally destroyed our marriage. It was bad enough for Jeff imagining that I might be with another man. The thought of my being with another woman was too much for him."

"Look, Holly, you're a good friend, a very good friend. That's all you'll ever be. You're a left-handed batter, and I'm not. Women do not attract me, at all. I appreciate all that you've done for me. I've had a wonderful experience here. Even so, I'm not interested in becoming your lover."

Despite everything, she insisted on driving me to the airport. At the gate, I kissed her on the cheek, then waved goodbye.

Chapter 12

When I returned to Mammoth Falls after my sojourn in California, the town hadn't changed much at all. Our old homestead was the same as it had always been. I found Momma in fine fettle. We stood together in the kitchen talking while the aroma of fried chicken made my mouth water.

"Momma, I'd like to stay here for a while, if that's okay."

"Of course, dear. What're your plans?"

"Well, I've decided to go back to college, either on that scholarship, if it's still available, or under the GI Bill. I think it's important for me to finish."

"Good for you, Ida Mae." She paused. "By the way, both Dodger and the pastor are dying to see you."

I stopped at Dodger's first. I could hear him strumming as I came up the front walk.

"Those are pretty good sounds I'm hearing," I said through the open door. I had spotted him in the living room.

"IDA MAE!" In another second, he was like a bear hugging me. "Let me look at you—the wandering troubadour. Are you here for any length of time?"

I gave him the story.

"Good," he said. "You can go to Woodstock with us."

"Woodstock?"

"Yes, it's a big thing, a huge concert in upstate New York at a place called Bethel."

"What dates?"

"August fifteen, sixteen, and seventeen."

"Who's going?"

"The entire band. Shooter is converting a large bus for resale and says we can use it for the trip."

"Where'll we stay?"

"On the bus—no other option. The concert will be in the middle of a huge field."

"Count me in. By the way, who's scheduled to play at the concert?"

When he told me, I was blown away.

"Go into the bedroom and arm yourself," he said. "I feel a duet coming on."

We played for an hour or so. By and by, he stopped.

"Oh, Ida Mae, you must know how I feel about you. Why don't you marry me and stay right here in Mammoth Falls?"

"Why, Dodger, you're very sweet. I love you, too, but I'm not *in love* with you. I can't be your wife, but I'll always be your friend."

"Ida Mae, you know how to break a guy's heart."

"While I'm at Pitt, we'll still have our gigs."

He looked at me with sad eyes.

"Dodger, are you going to be okay with this?"

When he began playing the wildest tune I'd ever heard, I knew he would be.

A half hour after seeing Dodger, I arrived at Pastor Highwater's office. He stood to hug me.

"Ida Mae, it's so good to see you." He pulled back to look into my eyes. "We all worried about you."

"I had some close calls, Pastor, but I'm still breathing."

"Take a seat," he said.

Now facing him as I sat across from him at his desk, he said, "What about romance?"

"There was a man in Vietnam. We planned to be married, but he was killed . . . which means I've lost two men to that war. There's nobody now, though."

"Ida Mae, the important issue is this: What have you learned from it all?"

"You know, Pastor, how do I say this?" I paused. "I'm completely changed because of the journey I've taken . . . in positive ways."

"That's good to hear. Tell me more."

"I've put my childish ways behind me. I can now see the importance of getting an education. After that, I want to pursue a career in music."

"Sounds like a good plan. I'm very proud of you."

Chapter 13

Our first task in preparing for Woodstock was to paint slogans and symbols on the bus. Our friend Shooter had parked it behind his gas station amidst used tires, empty oil cans, and auto parts to give us access to the high-pressure hose. Dodger used the hose to peel off the accumulated dirt, a necessary first step before any paint application. As the bus sat dripping in the sun, we sat on orange crates at the back entrance to the station.

"How far away is this place anyhow?" Shooter asked.

He had his arm around Sissy, a bleach-blonde about twenty-five years old.

"A little over six hundred miles," Dodger said.

"How long do you think it will take us?" Shooter asked.

"Depends on the roads. Depends on the traffic. But you can bet your family jewels that it will take significantly more than ten hours," Dodger said.

Sissy responded, "Ten hours! Ten hours! There's no way you're going to coop me up in that thing for ten-plus hours." She pointed at the bus.

I'd run into Sissy before. She wasn't my favorite person by any means. Well-endowed but cranky, she complained about everything. We had to put up with her because Shooter was a band member and Sissy was his girl.

"You're not going, then?" Dodger asked, looking at Sissy hopefully.

"I didn't say that. I just said I wouldn't like it," she said.

"How did they pick the concert location?" I asked, trying to change the subject.

"An interesting story—there's a town actually named Woodstock in upstate New York. The original plan was to hold it there. When the town fathers began to worry about the potential size of the crowd, the promoters switched it. The new spot is located at a place called Bethel about forty miles from the original site."

"Bethel sounds like something out of the Bible," I said.

"Yeah, I guess so, except the promoters decided to keep the original name—Woodstock," Dodger said.

"It's a cool name," Shooter said. "I can see why they kept it."

"The site covers about forty acres on a pig farm owned by a farmer named Max Yasgur," Dodger said.

"Oh great! A pig farm! We're going to a pig farm," Sissy said.

"Don't be a pain, Sissy," Dodger said, "or someone will bean you."

"Don't mouth me, you cocksucker," Sissy retorted.

Dodger raised his hands. "Nice talk," he said.

It was going to be a long trip with Sissy aboard. If Dodger didn't kill her, someone else certainly would. She hated me because she thought I was after Shooter. Nice as he was, he was just not attractive to me. Lanky and bowlegged, he had buck teeth and one tooth missing on each side. Even if his bad breath had been tolerable, no way I would ever go near him, as Shooter well knew. Still, Sissy hated me.

At that moment, Crowe showed up.

"Hey, Crowe, you're just in time. We haven't started painting yet," Dodger said.

"Glad to see you all," Crowe said. "An ice chest full of beer is in my trunk, which is open. Help yourselves."

"By the way," Dodger said, "all the expenses come out of the band fund, including Crowe's beer. We've got money for food. Ida Mae has offered to help with the buying. They're predicting a huge crowd at the site. I think the crowd is going to be bigger than they think."

"How big, Dodger?" Shooter asked.

"Don't hold me to it, but I wouldn't be surprised if a half million people showed up. Look at the talent that will be featured," he said, then rattled off the names.

"Good God almighty!" Crowe said.

"Dodger, how do you know so much about this event?" I asked.

"Simple. My cousin picked up a flyer in one of the record stores in New York City. Knowing of my interest in such things, he sent it to me. In my opinion, this will be one of the biggest musical events of the century," Dodger said.

"And we're going to be there," Shooter said.

"Yeah, if we ever make it in that thing," Sissy said, pointing at the bus.

Dexter, the last member of the band to show up, arrived at that point. He was an excellent base player who was loved by everyone who knew him. Smart and good-looking, he wrote most of our arrangements. His girlfriend, Mary Ann, who was as nice as Sissy was mean, accompanied him. She knew better than to think I would ever disrupt her relationship with Dexter.

Shooter had a weird sense of humor. Sneaking around behind the bus, he turned on the power blast and gave Dexter a shot before Dexter had a chance to react. In the process, he got some of the spray on Sissy.

"You lousy cocksucker," she screamed.

She didn't laugh, not at all. Neither did Dexter, who was soaked clear through.

Dexter went home to change. Not long after he returned, each of us began to assess our painting assignments. Mine being the hood, I decided to do a peace sign.

"How trite," Sissy said.

I ignored her.

Sissy decided to use the slogan *Make Peace Not War* along the entire length of the bus on the driver's side. Talk about trite. The others did flowers, large ones, in various colors, a psychedelic array.

"There we have it," Dodger said.

"Now we're flower children, pure and simple. We should buy a supply of drugs," Shooter said.

"Naw, beer's all we need," Dodger answered.

"If there's going to be any pill popping or syringes, I'm not going," Sissy said.

"There won't be," Dodger assured her.

"Hey, I just thought of something," Shooter said. "In many cases, the flower people convert Volkswagen vans. They call them 'vanovers.' Well, this here is a 'busover.' Yeah, that's it—we've got a busover." He smiled.

"Let's talk about the itinerary," Dodger said. "We want to be there a full day before the concert opens. We don't want to get caught in the crowd. Dexter, you're in charge of travel plans. You've got to figure how to get us there and back. Ida Mae, as we discussed, you're in charge of food. Figure food for four days. We can eat out while we're on the road."

"Who died and made you king?" Sissy asked.

"Somebody's got to be in charge, Sissy, and it might as well be me," Dodger said.

"Button your lip, Sissy. Dodger's the man," Dexter said.

"I agree," Shooter said.

"Me, too," said Crowe.

"You all know how I feel. And I've got a question, boss," I said.

"Fire away," Dodger answered.

"Where are we going to store the food? An ice chest won't be big enough," I said.

"Shooter has welded in a full-size refrigerator/freezer. Don't ask me how it works—something about car batteries or generators or pixie dust. I expect there will be ample room in there even with that crazy device. We'll also be taking ice chests," Dodger said.

"The refrigerator-freezer is welded in. Do you want me to tell you how it works?" Shooter asked.

Next followed a chorus of *nos*.

"Will there be concession stands?" I asked.

"Considering where this concert will be taking place, I don't think we can count on them. We've got to provide for our own existence," Dodger said.

"Not only that, but we've also got to count on the fact that there will be hungry people milling around. In addition to locking the front door when necessary, we should also be able to lock the door to the refrigerator-freezer, just in case," Dexter said.

"Another thing: Not all of us can sleep inside at the same time. We'll need to get a canopy or overhang to attach to the bus. We'll also need sleeping bags for all of us, and blankets. I'll take care of all of that," Dodger said. He paused. "Can anyone think of anything else?"

"I'm sure other things will come up, but what you've told us should get us started," I said.

The start date was four days away.

After I bought the food, I visited my old friend Bridget at her job. It was like taking a pilgrimage to the Oracle of Delphi, an appropriate course of action when a long trip is planned, I thought. It was also time for a hair and nail appointment.

"Woodstock—you're soooo lucky to be going," Bridget said as she worked on my nails.

"Why don't you come with us?" I asked.

"Impossible. I'm stuck to this job—like a French whore when the fleet is in," she said.

We laughed.

"Now tell me, Ida Mae, about your adventures."

"You mean about the men in my life, don't you?"

She smiled.

She already knew about Bleeder, so I told her about Hap and his untimely death. Then, I told her about my experiences in California.

"Those people are all crazy out there," she said.

"So true. They're doing things on a routine basis that we haven't even thought about yet. It was like being in never-never land. I was dying to get home."

She finished my nails. "Ida Mae, let me do your fortune," she said.

She got out the cards, shuffled them, and began setting them out one at a time.

"I continue to see good things for you. There'll be no man in your life for some time yet, but don't despair because something good is going to happen down the line."

"Well, it's about time."

"Oh, and there's one other thing. Something bizarre is going to happen during your trip to Woodstock."

"Should I cancel?"

"No, not at all, nothing like that. However, when it comes to bizarre events, this one will be at the top of the list."

"Can you tell me exactly what will happen?"

"Nothing definite is registering. Sorry."

I elected not to tell the gang about Bridget's premonition. There would be enough pressure on us with Sissy on board. It made no sense to add to it.

We planned to pack everything into the bus the night before. Hopefully, we'd be able to drive straight through. If we arrived on the fourteenth, that would put us there a full day before any of the festivities were scheduled to begin, giving us a chance to find a choice parking spot before the crowds descended.

On the day of our departure, everyone arrived on time, at five in the morning—Crowe, Dexter, Mary Ann, Sissy, Dodger, Shooter, and me. Once on the road, I began to feel confident that the bus would get us there and back. For the first several hours, we played and sang every song in our repertoire. By the time we got to Harrisburg, my voice was raw, not just from the singing but also from the cigarette smoke that Shooter and Sissy produced. With those two, one cigarette followed another in rapid succession until the butts were piled high in an ashtray the size of a garage can lid.

"You know, we're sounding damn good. It's too bad we're not on the program. We'd really wow 'em," Dodger said.

"How could they have passed us over?" Shooter laughed.

Dodger pulled into a parking lot beside a roadside restaurant and tavern. At that point, we were way behind schedule due to the persistent stops attributable to Sissy's weak kidneys.

"Sissy, I hope for your sake that the Woodstock planners remembered to include bathroom facilities," Dodger said as we sat down in a large booth.

"They damn well better if a half million people are going to be there," she said.

From the moment we walked into the restaurant, I could tell we weren't welcome. The patrons at the bar turned to glare at us. The waitress was surly. The three men playing pool in the back mumbled among themselves and then burst out laughing. At one point, I heard the phrase *goddamn hippies*.

"Dodger, there's going to be trouble," I whispered. "Let's get the hell out of here."

"Too late. They've cut us off," he said.

"But—"

"Trust me, Ida Mae. Here's what you do. Use the bathroom, then go outside like you forgot something. Once inside the bus, get my blue duffle bag. It's beside the front seat. Hide it under your coat and bring it to me. The bus is locked. Here are the keys."

Dodger paused. In high volume he called the bartender. "My good man, this young lady would like to use the facilities. Would you be so kind as to tell us where they are?"

The bartender sneered as he pointed toward the bathroom.

As I passed by, it struck me that the men in the bar and at the pool table looked like a pack of wolves—dirty, sinister, fiery-eyed. What little light was present in the room seemed to glint off the whites of their eyes. After standing in the bathroom for a few minutes, I walked back into the main room.

"Baby, you're a real knockout," the man at the door said.

"Excuse me," I said, "I've got to get something out of the bus."

"What do you have to get, sweetheart?"

"Well, my period just started a little early and my Tampax is—"

"Go ahead, but be quick about it," he snarled. Reluctantly, he stepped aside.

After finding the bag, I returned. When I entered, the man at the door bolted the front door behind me. The bartender reacted quickly but not before I had a chance to drop the bag near Dodger.

"I've got a great idea. Why don't we have some fun with these ladies? Right there on the pool table. Put a *closed* sign in the window, Simon," he said as he came around the bar to address Dodger. "You are the ugliest motherfucker I ever saw," he told him.

One thing I knew from watching Dodger in action following

one of our sets at the bar in Pittsburgh: You didn't use the word *ugly* in Dodger's presence. It put him into a rage. In a flash, he was on his feet brandishing the shiny revolver that he had removed from the bag I delivered. He put it against the bartender's temple.

"If you say one more word, shit-face, I'm going to blow your head off."

The man's eyes opened wide.

"Now, you tell that man over by the front door to unlock it—and I mean now!" Dodger said.

Suddenly, we were outside. While holding his victim in a chokehold, Dodger yelled at us to move quickly. "I'll cover you until you're all inside the bus. Then swing over here and pick me up." At the same time, he whispered something to Shooter.

"That was close," I said as we barreled up the highway. "One question—Dodger, what did you say to Shooter?"

"I told him to get the ice pick out of the toolbox and puncture holes in the tires of every vehicle in the parking lot behind the restaurant."

"It was easy," Shooter said. "The five motorcycles were parked side by side in the back lot."

"WHOOOEEE. They'll be roaring mad," I said.

"By the way, Ida Mae, you should have taken the time to load Big Bertha," Dodger said, pointing to the revolver.

"You mean—?"

"Yep. Sometimes a bluff's as good as a—"

"I don't think it's funny at all," Sissy interrupted. "I was almost a rape victim. I want to go home, and I want to turn back now!"

"Now, Sissy, calm your jets. We've come this far. Let's finish it. They'll be talking about Woodstock for generations," Mary Ann said.

"I agree," I said, "but I must admit that I was scared out of my wits, although I was excited, too. This will be something to remember, something we should finish."

Dodger chimed in. "Besides, if we go back, we'll have to pass the restaurant and face those hoodlums a second time."

"What if they come after us?" Crowe asked.

"They won't be able to do that for hours. And even if they start after us later, which they won't do, it'll be like finding a needle in a haystack in all those people. Besides, they were never given any details about our destination," Dodger said.

Shooter burst out laughing.

"What's so funny?" Mary Ann asked.

"I'm just remembering an incident in high school. We'd gone to an obscure town to watch a car rally. On the way back, we stopped at a bar. On a dare, I told Dodger that the guy behind the bar had said he was ugly, knowing how mad he got when anyone used that word." Shooter laughed again, then continued.

"Well, Dodger goes over to the bartender and asks, 'Did you say I was ugly?' The guy says, 'No, I didn't. But come to think of it, you are the ugliest son of a bitch I ever saw. *You're as ugly as the bottom of a shithouse.*' Well, when he said that, I knew we were in trouble. Dodger decked him with one punch, which prompted a guy behind Dodger to help his friend. As this guy spins Dodger around, Dodger takes the lead by giving this guy a hard right to the chin. The guy goes down like a bag of rags."

I noticed that Dodger wasn't laughing.

"By this time the bartender had gathered himself together. He came up from behind the bar with a shotgun. Dodger and the rest of us made a fast exit," Shooter said. He laughed again.

"Shooter, I wish you wouldn't tell those stories," Dodger said.

"I'll bet you do," Dexter said. "But I've got a story to tell as well. My story involves a different car rally and a different bar but a similar set of facts. Some guy looks at Dodger and starts barking like a dog. Dodger is really pissed, but this guy is with ten of his closest buddies, and there is only the three of us."

"What happened next?" Mary Ann asked.

"We left the joint at that point. Back then, Dodger always kept a box of war relics in his trunk. He went out to the car and got a disarmed hand grenade. Then, he went back to the open door of the bar and threw it in." Dexter laughed out loud. "Well, when the dummy grenade hit the floor, there was nothing but asses and elbows in that place. It cleared out so fast, you'd have thought it was a police raid. There were so many bodies piled up behind the bar and in the parking lot, it looked like a malfunction at a sausage factory."

"What happened next?" Mary Ann asked again, smiling.

"Well, I suppose they discovered it was a dud, but we were long gone by then," Dexter said.

"I wish you guys wouldn't tell those stories," Dodger said again.

That only made Shooter and Dexter and Crowe laugh harder.

Chapter 14

By seven o'clock that night, we were all dead tired and hungry. Dexter figured we were only about thirty miles from Bethel. We stopped at a trailer park he had seen advertised. In our assigned parking spot, we found a grill. We had our own grill, of course, but we concluded that using the outside grill would make things easier. Most important, there was a nearby public facility for taking showers.

"It may be the last shower we get in some time, so take advantage of it," Dodger said. "We'll eat here and spend the night. Tomorrow morning, we'll drive in early."

"We should have a leg up on the crowd," Crowe said.

I oversaw the cooking. Still, I enlisted Crowe's aide with the hamburgers and the buns while I kept an eye on the baked beans and corn. After the meal, everyone was full of compliments. Sissy said nothing. Nor had she offered to lift a hand.

The shower after dinner hit the spot. By the time I finished, the boys had the canopy rolled out and in place. It was comforting to have the covering even though there was no sign of rain. The hard part was blowing up the air mattresses, but Dodger made that easy with a device he had bought at Western Auto. Sissy and

Shooter drew the lucky straw, giving them the right to sleep in the bus. The rest of us slept in sleeping bags on air mattresses under the canopy.

When we arrived at the concert grounds the next day, very few people were around. We paid the eighteen dollars per person entrance fee and drove inside. As we expected, the concert area consisted of a large field crisscrossed by several makeshift roads. Crews were still working on the stage when our bus approached.

Dodger talked to one of the workers through the open side window. "Where's the best place to park this thing."

"You see that rise over there," a man said, pointing. "That's the ideal location. You'll be able to see the stage without being jostled to death by the crowd."

We parked the bus at the spot suggested, set out the canopy and the deck chairs, and waited. Locationwise, our hangout was perfect. Not only were we close to the stage, but we were also a short distance from a privy. We planned to sit on the bus roof until the concert began. As an assist in getting up there, we turned over a metal garbage receptacle and placed it at the back, where a partial ladder was located.

At five o'clock, people began streaming in. However, not until the following afternoon did the real rush begin. Thousands and thousands arrived—hippies, beatniks, Jesus freaks, antiwar protestors, pro-war activists, mystics, Muslims. Headbands of various colors over long, straight hair seemed to be the most popular outfit. Marijuana smoke wafted everywhere. As we passed to and from the privy, we could see strong evidence that hard drugs were also being consumed—empty syringes littered the ground.

It was a sea of humanity. We learned that the promoters had given up on requiring tickets after the front fence was trampled down. We also learned that the promoters were anticipating a crowd of half a million; the mass of attendees convinced us that they weren't far wrong. When traffic on nearby roads jammed to a halt, many abandoned their cars and walked the rest of the way.

"Pray it doesn't rain. If it rains, this place will be a quagmire," I said.

"Don't even think such thoughts, Ida Mae," Shooter said.

The concert was delayed, and, of course, it did rain on the first day. Richie Havens, the initial performer, did not start off until well after five p.m. because of various delays. On that first day, Ravi Shankar had to shorten his five-song set because of the downpour.

Through it all, the crowd kept growing. The noise it produced, a constant rumbling, never quieted and was occasionally punctuated by a scream or a shriek. Even so, there were enough huge speakers and sound devices around to cause the weakest voice to erupt. Eleven artists performed the first day, an array of talent that caused Sissy to twitch and complain after the fourth set.

"This is so horrible I can't stand it—rock, folk, blues rock, folk rock, jazz rock, Latin rock, psychedelic rock. Pretty soon, it will all begin to sound the same, but always loud," she said.

"Hang in there, Sissy, you've only got two more days to go," I said, laughing.

Saturday's program was even more ambitious. It included an all-night marathon featuring, among others, Janis Joplin, the Grateful Dead, Creedence Clearwater Revival, The Who, and Jefferson Airplane. Janis was outrageous, as usual. When she sang "Piece of My Heart," the crowd went wild. Well before the last performance, Sissy had disappeared inside the bus.

Because of the rain, deep mud was the order of the day. In time, cleanliness became a low priority. My third pair of jeans became caked with mud very quickly. Luckily, the bus roof temporarily freed us from the mud invasion, but only when it wasn't raining. Even so, our beer consumption caused many impromptu trips to the privy through that mess.

Late Sunday morning, we provided an impromptu concert of our own in front of the bus, which we were now calling *Maggie*. Because a lot of people were out of food, we offered free hot dogs. Mary Ann volunteered to do the cooking as we played and sang. Soon, a throng surrounded *Maggie*. I volunteered that their interest had more to do with the food than with the music.

On one of our breaks, I heard a voice: "IDA MAE!"

I looked toward the sound to see a woman waving at me frantically. As she came closer, I realized that it was Holly.

"I don't believe it . . . I don't believe it," I said.

We hugged.

"You don't think I'd miss the concert of the century, do you?" she asked.

"What about the shop?"

"Lu Lu can take care of things for a few days."

"Lu Lu?"

"She came on board right after you left."

Holly explained that she had financed the airfare for herself and two of her gay friends. They had flown into the closest city and rented a car, which at that moment was about two miles up the road in a ditch.

"We walked the rest of the way with everything we could carry. Luckily, the boys spotted some friends soon after we started walking. When we arrived, they offered shelter under a canopy like yours."

"How did you find me?"

"Just followed the sound of your music . . . had no idea you'd be here."

Remembering what Holly looked like in that exquisite gown of hers at the Academy Awards, her mud-soaked, makeupless appearance, completed with a plain green poncho over blue jeans, shocked me. Then I realized that I looked exactly the same.

"I'd like you to meet Jason and Bruce," she said.

When Holly spoke, both of her friends turned to greet me. They were very nice, but my initial impression was somewhat negative. Both had dyed blond hair and wore eyeshadow. They could have passed for twins. Thin and long-legged, they appeared to be immature adults of identical height who were just one or two genes away from being full-fledged albinos. Like Holly, they wore ponchos over blue jeans.

When I was done gaping, I introduced all three to my friends. As Holly, Jason, and Bruce tried our hot dogs, we began another informal set unconnected in any way to the performances on stage.

Not until two o'clock did Joe Cocker start things off again. His selections—"Let's Go Get Stoned," "With a Little Help from My Friends," "Delta Lady," and others—whipped the crowd into a frenzy. Unfortunately, a storm disrupted the schedule for several hours after Cocker's set finished. We all sat under the canopy with the intention of waiting it out.

Dodger brought out three wooden benches, and we spread ourselves out on them. Holly, Jason, and Dodger occupied one, Dexter, Mary Ann, and I were on the another, and Shooter, Crowe, Sissy, and Bruce sat on the third.

Jason interrupted our reverie. "If you're interested in gossip, we've got it. For some unknown reason, everyone in the crowd wants to share tidbits with us."

"Like what?" Shooter asked.

"Like three deaths happened here on these grounds," Jason said.

"Go on," Shooter said.

"One poor fellow died when a tractor rolled over him while he was sleeping in a field in his sleeping bag," Jason said.

"And the others?" Dodger asked.

"Drug overdoses," Jason said.

"A tough way to go," Shooter said.

"But it evens out," Bruce said.

"How so?" I asked.

"Two births," Bruce answered.

"No kidding? Right here in the field?" I asked.

"I assume so," Bruce said.

"You people certainly came a long way. California is way out there," Dexter said.

"I can't understand why anyone would want to live in California," Sissy said, "with all those gays and the drugs."

"Have you ever been there?" Jason asked.

"Of course not," Sissy answered.

"Then don't you think you should keep your fucking mouth shut about it?" Jason said.

"Now wait a minute," Shooter said.

"Hold on, Shooter," Dodger said. "Jason here wasn't out of line. That girl of yours has been shooting off her mouth since this trip began. She was being plain rude to this man by giving an opinion that wasn't called for."

"I've never been so humiliated in all my life," Sissy puffed as she walked toward the bus.

Shooter was staring daggers at Dodger.

"Careful, Shooter, or you and your bitch will be walking the hell out of here on your own," Dodger said.

"You're forgetting that I own this bus," Shooter said. He then turned quickly and went inside.

For the rest of us, that short outburst seemed to clear the air. We talked freely for the remainder of the afternoon while the rain pelted against the awning above our heads. During that interval, we ate grilled chicken *à la* Dodger. Shooter and Sissy showed up to get their share and then disappeared back inside. Black curtains neatly placed over the windows gave them the privacy they seemed to be looking for. After the rain stopped, Dodger laid out some of the mattresses on the roof and we all climbed up top. Holly sat beside me.

"I'll never forget this," she said. "I'm so glad we came."

"And you should be proud of yourself for sticking to beer. Blow can be wicked stuff," I said.

"What do you think I've been doing in the privy." She laughed.

Country Joe and the Fish resumed the concert at six p.m. Other groups followed. Blood, Sweat & Tears ushered in the midnight hour. Crosby, Stills, Nash & Young began about three a.m. Sha Na Na then played "Book of Love" and "Duke of Earl," two favorites out of my past. Jimi Hendrix, who was supposed to conclude the concert at midnight, didn't even begin his set until nine a.m. Belting out at least sixteen songs, he provided a fantastic ending performance. By then, many of the onlookers had begun to leave.

When Jimi finished, Holly leaned in close to speak to me. "Ida Mae, I'm so glad I had a chance to see you again." She paused. "You know, you can still have a home with me anytime you choose."

"You've made that very clear to me, Holly, and I appreciate your offer very much."

"But you're not inclined to take me up on it."

"No, my home is here in the East. And some day I will marry here, I hope."

"So be it! And now let's talk about more practical things. We need a ride to our rental car. Can you provide it?"

"Of course," I answered.

It was tight. Packed into *Maggie* were Holly and her two friends along with the six of us. Shooter had done an excellent job customizing the vehicle before the trip began. Having removed all original seats, except for the driver's seat, he had expanded the space and then added seating along each wall, broken up by the refrigerator and certain storage cabinets. In the back end, the wooden benches that were outside were now placed side by side to form a bedframe of sorts. The idea was to support two mattresses on that platform.

Rather than be caught in a traffic jam, we waited several hours before leaving. By the time we departed, most of the attendees had cleared out. Dodger drove to the front gates, and we pulled the curtains back so that we could study our surroundings. The place looked like a battlefield.

Debris lay everywhere. Most of the grass had turned into mud, and the mud gave evidence of thousands of footprints. We saw things like old tennis shoes and broken guitar parts and sunglasses and drug paraphernalia of all sorts and empty beer cans, thousands of them, everywhere, and empty boxes and newspapers and bits of food and discarded clothing.

"Well, Sissy, are you going to talk to us or not?" Dexter asked as we pulled onto the main road.

"I suppose so," she said, smiling coyly.

"Attagirl," Shooter said. "My last girlfriend would hold a grudge forever. Sometimes, she wouldn't talk to me for months. You guys remember Zena, don't you?"

"How could we forget Zena," Dodger said. "We called her 'The Princess of Darkness.'"

We all laughed.

"Well, Zena could hit the bottle pretty good. One night she had had too much to drink. We were at Pappy's in Mammoth Falls. When I told her she better not have another drink, she had a quick retort: *You're just being stubborn because I told everyone you were a lousy lay.*"

We all laughed again.

"I broke up with her right after that," Shooter said, still laughing.

It wasn't long after that that the bus lurched suddenly to the right, throwing all of us from our seats. We looked at Dodger as he struggled to get the bus back on the road. The passenger-side front and back wheels had apparently gone off the shoulder onto soft ground. We could hear gravel and dirt being kicked upward as Dodger gunned the gas. Eventually, Dodger gave up and pulled into a clearing on the right side of the road.

When the bus stopped, Dodger slumped over the wheel and began to wail. "Oh, God, God, God! I saw him, right out in the middle of the road, facing me," he said.

"Who, Dodger? Who did you see?" I asked.

"It was him. I know it was him. Swerved to miss him. Went off the road."

Dodger's forehead was covered with perspiration, his eyes wide.

Shooter left the bus to look outside, then came back in. "Dodger, there's nobody out there. I could see for two hundred yards in both directions. There was nothing."

"Who did you see, Dodger?" I asked again.

"I've seen pictures of him—the beard, the beret. It was Che Guevara. He was standing in the middle of the road, armed to the teeth."

Jason, Holly's friend from the Coast, stepped forward. "Look, Dodger, I happen to be a shrink. Let me ask you a few questions," he said.

"I'm shaking I'm so rattled," Dodger admitted.

"Do you have times when you feel very low, depressed?" Jason asked.

"God, yes, all the time. If it wasn't for my music I'd—"

"And at other times, you feel high, very positive, fully in charge, invincible?"

"How did you know?"

"I've been studying you. This incident is very important."

"What does it tell you?" Dodger asked.

"I suspect that you're manic-depressive. That would be my diagnosis."

"I'm what?"

"Manic-depressive. It's also known as bipolar disease. Your mood swings are caused by a chemical imbalance. I speculate that the large amount of beer consumed over the past few days brought on what the specialists call a 'hypomanic episode.' You thought you saw Che Guevara, but you didn't. You hallucinated."

"He looked awfully real to me."

"That's understandable," Jason said. "However, I know something about Guevara. He was killed in Bolivia in 1967. He couldn't have been standing on the road because he's dead."

"Let's assume I have this disease you're talking about. Can you help me?"

"Absolutely. The first step is to get you lined up with a shrink in your area. I can do that for you. The next step is to get the right medication through that person. The medication will keep you in balance."

"What kind of medication?"

"Probably lithium, plus an antidepressant." Jason continued his inquiry. "Tell me what you're feeling when the depression hits."

"Have you ever gotten a good look at me? I'm as ugly as an ostrich's ass. I'm doomed to be alone for life. Every now and then, that realization hits me."

"If that's your demon, you've got to learn to live with it or release it," Jason said.

"Dodger," I said, "I'm beginning to think that the vision on the road was the best thing that could have happened to you, particularly with Jason here to help you."

"Not only that," Bruce said. "Holly, Jason, and I come from never-never land, where plastic surgery is a routine practice. There is no reason to despair about your looks. A little tuck here, a little snip there and you'll be looking like William Holden."

"Please don't mess with me. I know I'm pug ugly. I haven't been laid in years."

"In California, everyone gets plastic surgery. They can fix your jaw. They can fix your teeth. They can improve your appearance tenfold. And at some point, you'll have to go on a diet. They'll probably recommend that you lose fifty pounds or more. It can be done," Bruce said.

Holly added a comment. "I had a little work done a year or so ago . . . wanted to get rid of my chicken neck."

"Is it expensive?" Dodger asked.

"You bet your sweet ass it's expensive," Bruce said.

We all laughed.

We dropped Holly, Bruce, and Jason at their car. At the end of our visit together, I ended up liking her two friends immensely. They cared. I embraced each one separately. Jason made the referral when he got back to LA. And Dodger went on a diet and began to put money away for a face job.

I returned to school in the fall. The best part of it: I could room with Connie as before. She was now beginning her junior year. In those days, everyone seemed to have a negative opinion about the war. Throughout the time I was there, the Pitt campus remained a hotbed of protest.

Things happened somewhat predictably in my life after returning to Pitt. I received my undergraduate degree and then went on to get a master's in English followed by a PhD. I accepted a professorship in the English Department at Gannon College in Erie, Pennsylvania.

Chapter 15

After some years, I met the man of my dreams, Dennis Spencer, a Robert Redford lookalike who came to Gannon to teach economics. By then, the students had put me in the "spinster" category since I was in my early thirties with no romantic prospects in the offing.

Dennis and I met in the campus library, where an unplanned conversation behind the stacks on the poetry floor led to an invitation to dinner at the Taco Tree on campus. Our mutual interest in poetry was the key attraction for both of us, and before long we were sharing and discussing each other's work. The difference was that he had three self-published books of poetry under his belt whereas I'd never attempted to publish anything.

Following an informal dinner, Dennis and I were in the living room of my apartment sipping wine when he said, "Ida Mae, you've got to come out of your shell. I've read several of your poems, and they are very good."

"Publishable?"

"I think so, yes."

"You're not serious?"

"I *am* serious. Let me read to you one of my favorites.

Hearing the words read may help you recognize its exceptional quality . . . a different slant, that sort of thing."

He began to read.

FOXFIRE

You are foxfire,
a rare luminescence
seen on boggy ground,
a will-o'-the-wisp
that is present, then gone,
only to reappear further on.
I would like to marry you,
to hold you,
but you slip quickly
through my fingers
like cold water
on a hot day.
How can I love a dragonfly?
I never know
where next you will light.
I might just as well
duplicate a hummingbird's
cruising speed
or kiss a butterfly in flight.

"Let me assure you that this poem qualifies for the top ranks."

"You're too kind. The problem with the poem is that it's written from a man's viewpoint. It doesn't work for me."

"You're flat wrong on that score. The poem sings whether it comes from a male voice or a coat rack. And listen to this one."

NEVER ALONE IN A CEMETERY

Never alone
in a cemetery,
I walk
down Millionaire's Row
whose members
are just as quiet,
dead silent,
as the common folk.

There are no dolmens,
menhirs or cromlechs here.
And the obelisks,
rare as they are,
do not compare
to the massive monoliths of old
that once raged out of the ground.

But the same starlings
our ancestors saw,
hundreds and hundreds of them,
still startle *en masse*
to pulverize the winter sky,
before alighting once more,
dead black,
upon each silhouetted limb,
eternally.

"You hit the jackpot a second time with that one."
"Dennis, you're embarrassing me. You just want to get me hot from all the praise so you can get me into bed."
The conversation went silent at that point. After several

seconds, Dennis turned to me and smiled. "Well, that's true as hell, but that isn't the only reason why I—"

He didn't finish the sentence because in a matter of seconds, I was standing in front of him totally naked. He picked me up and carried me into my bedroom, where he showed me the full extent of his admiration, and poetry had very little to do with it.

By that summer, I was married and pregnant.

By this time, Bridget had long ago left the business at the hair salon in Mammoth Falls and taken up with a colony of Spiritualists in Lily Dale, in New York. Years before, when she had determined that Lily Dale was a short drive away from Gannon College, the prospect of joining the group gripped her.

Now, Bridget had a thriving "second sight" business in Lily Dale. She would simply close her eyes and could foresee people's futures. She had done so well by way of customers that she had been able to buy a cottage in town and when the time came, she had the money to follow her fellow soothsayers to their winter quarters in Sarasota, Florida. Eventually, she bought a second cottage there.

One summer night, we were at Bridget's place in Sarasota sitting around a stone fireplace in her backyard. Beyond the muted glare of the fire, it was pitch-black, but we could hear the pounding of the surf a short distance away.

Dennis was staring intently into the fire.

"You know, the sound of the surf in the distance always makes me think of 'Dover Beach,'" he said.

"Where the hell is that? Never heard of it," Bridget said.

"At one point, it was in the mind of Matthew Arnold, a British poet who died long, long ago," he said.

"Tallyho, the poet emerges," I said, laughing.

"With that single poem, Arnold tops anything I could ever do. I had it totally memorized at one point, but because of this graying head of mine I can only remember the last few lines." He proceeded to recite them.

> Ah, love, let us be true
> To one another! For the world, which seems
> To lie before us like a field of dreams,
> So various, so beautiful, so new,
> Hath really neither joy, nor love, nor light,
> Nor certitude, nor peace, nor help for pain.
> And we are here as on a darkling plain
> Swept with confused alarms of struggle and flight,
> Where ignorant armies clash by night.

"Talk about bringing down the black curtain," Bridget exclaimed.

"It's Matthew Arnold's curtain, not mine," Dennis interrupted.

We all laughed.

A few months later, Dennis and I were blessed with the birth of our first child, a son whom we named Adrian for no good reason.

Because of various conflicts, our next Sarasota trip to Bridget's place didn't happen until Adrian's fifth birthday. By that time, Connie and Hal, the man Connie had married, had become regulars on our Sarasota sojourn. But this year, they had to back out at the last minute.

Without the two of them, we tried unsuccessfully to capture the usual carefree mood that we associated with the Florida trips; but a pallor overtook us. The next day, it was augmented when Bridget unexpectedly fell into one of her trances, which until then had essentially abated.

We were seated on the patio in daylight when she began to spout. For the most part, her words were garbled and meaningless except for a few key phrases toward the end that shocked us mightily. As she spoke, she kept looking straight ahead with unseeing eyes.

"One day, Adrian will be involved in a murder, an event that will rock his very soul. It will be tragic for him and for your family generally."

Abruptly recovering her senses, she remained silent. We could only hear the incessant surf.

I spoke first. "Bridget, you've really done it this time."

We gave her the details.

"I've always felt that one murder in the family was one murder too many," I said.

"So sorry," she said. "It just comes. I can't control it."

From that moment forward to the end of our visit, she never recanted or attempted to adjust the wording of her alarming prophecy. We left Sarasota in a rattled condition that eliminated all conversation for the first fifty miles.

Many months later, Connie called to suggest a new place for our next vacation. She had spent time in Chautauqua Institution as a child and said that we should try it out, adding that it was in the same general area in New York where Lily Dale and Gannon were located. Dennis and I agreed that it seemed like a logical choice.

We all enjoyed our stay there so much during our first summer that we decided to buy a cottage there together. A year had passed since we last saw Bridget, who hadn't left Sarasota. In fact, she had become a veritable recluse and informed us that she'd decided to stay in Florida permanently. When we asked her to become a part owner of the Chautauqua cottage, she declined to join in the buy and made it very clear that her New York days were over.

As for us cottage owners, we settled on trading summer months—Adrian, Dennis, and me in July, and Connie and Hal in August, with a weekend overlap for both families in between.

PART II

Chapter 16

My name is Adrian. I am the only child of Dennis and Ida Mae Spencer. Early on, I became a big fan of Chautauqua Institution, where my family spent many wonderful summers. Chautauqua is a gated "summer colony" on Chautauqua Lake in New York. Mom and Dad co-owned a cottage on the grounds along with Aunt Connie and Uncle Hal.

The cottage, with its outside clapboard siding and log interior, was complemented by an oversized stone fireplace. The fireplace was most inviting on cool summer evenings, but I didn't like having to keep it clean and stocked with wood, which were the chores that fell to me.

I soon discovered that our cottage was only a short distance from Bestor Plaza, where a young crowd would gather most evenings around a concrete fountain that spewed water from four corners. Soon after dinner, kids, all under fifteen, would meet at assigned spots around the base of the fountain and remain there until dark. The fountain stood in the center of a spacious grass quadrangle surrounded by a bookstore, an ice cream parlor (called the Refectory), a library, and a post office.

The year of the "rat incident" stands out in my mind even

now. It wasn't my first Chautauqua vacation, but it certainly was the most memorable. Our cottage had a second set of stairs that descended from the master bedroom down to the kitchen. That summer, Dad and Uncle Hal agreed that the burnt-out lighting in the stairway had to be replaced because the area, even during the daytime, would become pitch-dark. Dad had purchased the replacement fixtures but hadn't yet installed them.

For Mom, these extra stairs provided a shortcut to the kitchen. One afternoon while descending, she stepped on something. A high-pitched squeak left no doubt as to what it was. The hairy vagrant had remained unseen in the dark, a presence made even more unpleasant because of Mom's practice of going barefoot before locating and donning her slippers in the kitchen. Her loud screams and word choice have been described on many occasions:

"FUCK... IT'S A FUCKING RAT... AGGGHHHHHH... MY GOD!"

No one dared speak of the incident at dinner that evening. Throughout the icy silence, Mom glared at Dad with a look that could cut glass. Her reaction obviously made him think twice about applying a humorous summary, which was his usual practice. Mom was suffering from a mild case of post-traumatic stress attributed to what she regarded as Dad's negligence in failing to install the replacement lighting in a timely fashion. (By the way, no one ever discovered what happened to the rat. Dad bought a large trap the size of a siege catapult. It produced no results, which convinced him that our visitor had probably departed for better pickings.)

On my bike ride to Bestor Plaza the night of the incident, I laughed out loud, convinced that Mom would eventually see the humor in what had happened. As I pulled up to the site, I spotted the regular group of teens my age on the side of the fountain closest to the post office, our allotted space. I was shy and always found socializing difficult, so when I noticed a gorgeous creature in the group, I couldn't get up the gumption to approach her.

As it got darker, I got the impression she would be leaving soon when several young men gathered around her, obviously hoping she'd choose one of them to take her home. Then, suddenly, she turned toward me.

"I want *him* to take me home," she said, pointing.

I felt the air go out of my lungs, but I managed to take a step toward her. She was blonde with emerald-green eyes and with a shapely figure contained in a blue sweatshirt and dark-brown shorts. Her queue of admirers parted to let me through as I moved in her direction.

On the way to her cottage, she told me her name: Margo. She probably sensed that I was a social boob because in all sweetness she encouraged these words out of me—*a teenager, your exact age, here with my family, from Pittsburgh, no girlfriend.* When we got to the cottage porch, she sat down on the couch swing.

"Would you like to sit for a moment?"

I attempted to sit down beside her only to discover that the swing swung back as I tried to plant myself. The loud crash prompted her mother to ask about injuries as she peeked through the kitchen screen door. I assured her that I was okay, and Margo was very gracious about offering a hand to help me up. To make matters worse, once I was settled on the swing, I elected to tell her about the rat incident.

"I hate rats," she said when I finished. "I don't even like to talk about them."

I took the hint and changed the subject, but it was too late. The rat story had thrown cold water on our budding relationship. A few minutes later, she told me that she'd better go in. Naturally, I didn't try to kiss her.

On the way home, I trashed myself. *"Dork, dork, dork. I'm a complete dork. She obviously liked me, and I blew it. Why couldn't I have chosen a more agreeable topic, like dog feces?"*

From then on, when I saw her on the grounds, she made mincing noises and brought her hands up in front of her nose like a rat might do. Each time, I'd become thunderstruck and she would burst into laughter. I don't know how I got up the nerve to do it, but I asked her to a concert at the Amphitheater. Surprisingly, the date went extremely well. There was no talk of rats.

Later, I took her to a Fourth of July dance at the High School Club located in a building beside the lake. We were sitting after dark on a permanent bench facing the water some distance from an upstairs dance floor that offered a piano's faint tinkling. The lakeside cottage owners had placed red flares on their properties, which made it appear as if a crimson necklace surrounded the lake. Even though she had placed a sweater around her shoulders, I could feel her shiver as we sat at the water's edge. I put my arm around her.

"Isn't it wonderful?" Margo said.

"Wonderful is the right word," I answered.

The lake appeared to be still, like a darkened mirror, but a gentle lapping sound nearby belied what our eyes were telling us and thousands of stars provided a cosmic overlay as though the universe was giving its approval. I took her hand, knowing that I was about to kiss her.

Chapter 17

My mother used to say, *"Adrian has trouble stepping out of the spotlight once it focuses on him,"* or something like that. What she meant was that as a ham, I tend to pile one story on top of another as a bid for attention, admittedly a correct assessment. As shy as I was with women, however, it amazed her and me that I adopted this practice.

Out of the blue, Bridget invited me to visit her in Sarasota one summer. When Mom told me about the offer, I was, at first, reluctant to accept it. I knew Bridget only by reputation—I didn't remember much about her from the family trip to Sarasota when I was five—and the account I'd received presented her as being somewhat "different."

"Adrian, you'll hurt her feelings if you refuse," Mom said.

Tough as Bridget was by reputation, I couldn't imagine her having hurt feelings about anything, but I relented.

The first problem was how to get me down there. Being only sixteen, I couldn't fly alone. It turned out that Dad had business in Florida, so he flew down with me. He had to catch a second flight and left me alone to meet Bridget at a prearranged location.

When I spotted her, she was holding a small dog. Right off, I learned that the dog's name was Chezette, a nasty little miniature poodle that didn't like me anymore than I liked her. To make her position totally clear, the dog tried to bite me as I leaned in to hug Bridget.

"Now, sweetie, you'll love Adrian," Bridget said to the dog. "He's here to visit us."

Chezette growled at me, showing her teeth. On the way to the cottage, she sat on her mistress's lap and put her ugly little dog face out the window on the driver's side. From time to time, she turned and glared at me as if to say, *"This lady is mine, so you'd better keep away."*

Aunt Bridget's deep affection for the dog was painfully evident. Chezette's nails were painted red, a procedure that obviously required much patience and skill. Soon, I discovered that the dog ate her food at the table. I mean *on* the table. At all other times, she was in Bridget's arms or lap. Her mistress kept kissing her or baby-talking to her. At first, it appeared that Aunt Bridget loved the dog so much that she was unable to part with her even for a short time. Then I spotted the *door*.

"I see that Chezette comes and goes as she pleases."

"You're talking about the doggie door. It has worked out very well. Chezette loves the freedom it gives her. I have to pick up droppings in the backyard from time to time, but I don't mind."

"I can do that for you while I'm down here, Aunt Bridget."

"That would be very nice, dear. One rule is important, though: Always keep the back gate closed. Otherwise, she'll run into the lake, and I'm not sure she knows how to swim."

By contrast, Aunt Bridget was an avid swimmer. She got up early most mornings "to take a dip." The water was deep enough to accept her flat dive off the dock, but just barely. As for me, my dislike of water sports of any type prompted a refusal to all entreaties.

It was not just Chezette that rubbed me the wrong way. In the short time I was visiting, I'd developed a strong dislike for the entire state of Florida. The days were unbearably hot, and just when you thought it couldn't get any hotter, it always did. After three days, I was beginning to look and feel leathery.

Another shortcoming was the architecture. The houses around the lake seemed identical. In my mind, they fit into the Florida formula of giving every house a made-of-plastic look, and I wasn't surprised to spot plastic flamingos in several of the yards.

On this day, the blue sky showed no clouds. I assumed they had been burned away by the intense heat that caused a shimmering brightness on the surface of the lake. Except for the faint buzz of a single hedge clipper three houses up, all was quiet.

On the patio, I was engrossed in *Huckleberry Finn*, a book assigned by my English teacher for summer reading. Aunt Bridget had gone to the Piggy Wiggly, which didn't allow dogs, even little ones. Because it was too hot to leave Chezette in the car, Aunt Bridget had assigned her to my care. Thankfully, the dog remained inside the house while I was reading, assuring me of the isolation I desired. I was lying on a chaise.

As much as I tried, I couldn't get through the last few chapters of *Huckleberry Finn*. From the moment Tom Sawyer arrived on the scene, the story went downhill. Convinced that Twain was off his feed at the end, I closed the book and set it down. In no time, I was asleep.

Abruptly, Chezette's barking woke me up. It's what I often called *"a little doggie bark,"* doubly annoying because of its high pitch. Having spotted something from her perch at the kitchen window, she was through the doggie door, over the patio, up the brick walk, through the open gate, and onto the dock, yapping all the way.

Chezette's barking made me stand up to see what was disturbing her. To my horror, I realized that I'd left the gate open. At the same moment, I saw a huge alligator gliding effortlessly toward the dock. I shouted at Chezette to come back, but, of course, she ignored me. She had a better plan. She stood, tiny and defiant, at the end of the dock while facing the sinister presence that was slowly gliding toward her. Later, when I thought back on the scene, I imagined a menacing grin on the alligator's long snout.

I watched transfixed as the beast placed its snout partially under the dock, and then I was jolted further by the watery explosion as the dock crashed upward flipping Chezette into the air. Her forward motion caused her to roll into a graceful somersault that was destined to end badly. The beast's jaws were open, waiting. There was a final yelp from Chezette as she realized what her fate would be, followed by a gigantic splash and then silence.

It all happened so quickly. I stood frozen with my mouth agape. It soon dawned on me that Chezette's ugly demise wouldn't be favorably received by her mistress.

At first, I tried to compose a plan that would explain the dog's absence. I decided that I'd tell Aunt Bridget that Chezette had been kidnapped—three men with guns drawn had appeared out of nowhere. To back up the story, I even considered cutting letters out of newsprint to form a ransom note.

On second thought, I decided that Aunt Bridget was much too smart to fall for a ruse like that and decided to come clean. Too soon, I heard her car pulling into the gravel driveway. Then, I heard the kitchen door opening.

"Where's Chezette?"

I couldn't help myself. I told her everything, down to the look of terror on Chezette's little face just before she was devoured. What happened next amazes me to this day. Aunt Bridget began to laugh.

"I . . . can just see . . . your expression . . . when, when . . . Chezette . . . took her final dive."

Between fits of laughter, she pointed out that her dog must have had a death wish.

"If I were you . . . I wouldn't feel at all guilty . . . about any of it, including the open gate."

Aunt Bridget stopped to catch her breath, then continued to laugh at regular intervals.

"I'll tell you . . . one sure thing . . . though, I'll never . . . go swimming in that lake . . . again. Tomorrow . . . I'm joining the local health club. I . . . can . . . also . . . assure you . . . that my next dog will be a mastiff."

With that, I joined her laughter.

Not surprisingly, right up to the day Aunt Bridget died, she never again invited me to visit her. I was delighted. Florida was never my cup of tea. And she never got a mastiff either despite her promise to do so. Instead, she purchased another miniature poodle. The new dog, known as Butter Cup, turned out to be ten times meaner than Chezette. I was introduced to her only once when Bridget flew north to visit. Butter Cup was a devil dog with nasty little teeth that drew blood every time she sank them into my ankles.

Chapter 18

It was my junior year at Delphic College in Ohio. The fall term was just beginning. Mom and Dad had dropped me off at the frat house. A few of my frat brothers were making joyful noises in the parking lot beneath my room, located on the top floor of Sigma Chi. They were showing the enthusiasm that comes with the return to college for the fall semester. From the third floor, I could see what was happening below by stepping through the open window in my room onto the fire escape.

"Who's making all that racket down there?" I shouted.

The answer: Sniffer, Squirrel, Hippo, and Zorro. In most instances, no one could figure out how the fraternity nicknames came to be, but once in place, they remained fixed forever. My own, Cezno, made absolutely no sense. No longer was I known as Adrian. Oh, there were some nicknames such as Red Bush and Hooker whose meanings could be surmised, but for the most part the recipient was as much in the dark as any subsequent onlooker would be.

"Oh, look, there's Cezno." Zorro was pointing up at me.

"Hi, Cezno," said another, standing next to Zorro.

Then I heard a voice behind me. "Be careful out there."

It was Teflon, my roommate. He was standing in the room on the other side of the open window. I stepped inside. We shook hands. I spoke first.

"How was your summer, Tef?"

Despite his dark good looks, Teflon never seemed to attract women. He was probably too intelligent for most of them or too wild. After a few drinks, he would become boisterous, insulting, and belligerent. Women seemed to be unwilling to spend any time with him at all—which made his nickname *Teflon* seem appropriate.

"Cezno, have you ever been to Peoria in the summer?"

"No."

"Then don't ask."

Teflon was the smartest man I knew, with an intuition to match. He seemed to know what I was thinking before I did. The crewcuts he favored gave him a look somewhere between a college professor and a truck driver. No doubt, I believed, he would someday become the best trial lawyer or stockbroker or investment banker in New York City or anywhere else he decided to settle. I envied his potential. He became the person to whom I deferred from the moment we first met, even though I was taller and stronger.

"Cezno, my boy, it's good to be back. This semester, I'm going to bring this campus to its knees."

"Good for you, Tef. I'll be lucky to get through with my ass in place. Milton and the Seventeenth Century—can you imagine?"

While I majored in English, Teflon majored in economics—and he was quick to point out that there wasn't much I could do after college as an English major except flip hamburgers.

The Delphic campus was dry, but Tef paid little attention. He always had a beer can in hand inside the frat house. Alone, most nights he would drive about five miles to Neville, Ohio, for beers at Tony's Bar while I studied in the room. Neville was known for its bars, especially Tony's.

Despite his penchant for blowing off his daily studies, Tef crammed like a madman for final exams. One peculiarity of his drove me nuts: He always crammed alone in our room. After placing the textbook on the dresser, he would strut like a bandleader, reciting the text out loud until he learned it. At those times, I preferred studying in the library.

My irritation lessened when I began dating Dana, who insisted that I study with her, most often in the library. When the brothers elected me president of the house, I was sure they had made a huge mistake, but Dana assured me I was the man for the job.

Midway through junior year, Tef began to show the effects of his constant drinking. By that time, he was pouring Scotch into the can on top of the beer "to give it more punch," he said. However loud he had been before this change, he became even louder afterward.

His vocal powers became especially evident when certain of the alums asked for a reconsideration of a decision the actives made during rush. We had passed over a candidate, a "legacy" whose father had paid for a new kitchen the year before. In the cold light of day, after the fast pace of rush had ended, some of the brothers, including me, began to see the error of our ways.

I called a special meeting to deal with the subject. Unfortunately, Billy Conway's father showed up just as the actives were gathering to discuss the question. Billy was a fraternity brother who was also a legacy. Obviously, Mr. Conway's intention was to be present upstairs as we "adjusted" our decision. My initial inclination was to please the alums, but I could see that the presence of Conway's father would be a deterrent.

"Tef, do you have a comment?" I asked, pointing the gavel at my roommate. As usual, he was holding a can of beer as he stood up.

"Sure as hell I do. Are we men or mice? Old man Conway is upstairs right now trying to railroad the vote. I for one won't have any part of it." As his voice reached heroic proportions, he raised the beer can in the air. Then he adjusted to a more reasonable volume. "We gave this kid the old blackball fair and square. He didn't pass muster, and now the alums want us to take it back. Well, I refuse. If this kid becomes a pledge, I'm out of here!"

With that, he sat down acknowledging the cheers and hoots and thunderous applause prompted by his speech. Aware of my position on the matter, Tef had elected to defy his own roommate and close friend, and he had done so quite effectively. His speech turned the tide. Those who spoke in opposition were hissed at and booed. It was the scenario that every fraternity president most dreaded—to be blindsided by a "friend" in a chapter meeting.

I wasn't anxious to give my rebuttal, but I did it anyway.

"Hold it! The kid's as qualified as any other candidate. Yes, he's a legacy, but some of our best men have been legacies. Unfounded defiance is okay for kindergarten, but not here. And don't forget the new kitchen his father built for us last year."

It was no use. When young men get their backs up, as occurred on that day, the result is always explosive. The part that hurt the most was that Tef was leading the charge. Because of him, I was forced to accept the proposition that another president—a stronger president—might have put things right, something I had failed to do.

After that day, my relationship with Tef cooled down even further. It wasn't too noticeable at first because neither one of us spent much time together in the room. I was usually with Dana, and Tef was usually off somewhere drinking. As time passed, the coolness turned to ice.

Milton became a great source of relief. It wound up being an excellent class. Best of all, that's where I had first spotted Dana, a new sophomore—a knockout with a beautiful face and figure to match. It wasn't long before we began dating, and not long after that she became my pin-mate.

The Sweetheart Dance is a Sig function that occurs in the spring. Since the beginning of time, the Sig president's pin-mate automatically became the Sweetheart in any given year, except that Tef and a few others decided that the honor shouldn't be given to Dana because they didn't like her.

The night of the dance was a disaster, particularly when Zorro announced the new Sweeheart's name, something everyone knew ahead of time anyway. To survive the night, Dana and I drank too much. Later in my room, by myself, still inebriated, I went through an elaborate incantation.

"Teflon, I curse you. I curse you for all eternity."

Of course, I didn't mean a word of it, but when a man delivers a curse like that, even when drunk, it can't be taken back. After all, a hex is a hex.

It happened a month later. Tef had been drinking in Neville all day. Sissy, a Kappa, and Stretch, a frat brother who was also a football player, had accepted a ride with Tef back to the campus. Tef had seats available in his black Chevy, a wreck of a car. Sissy sat between the two men in the front seat. Suddenly, Tef, in a fit of drunken exuberance, elected to pass on a hill. The resulting head-on collision killed Stretch outright and permanently disabled Sissy. Tef survived, but just barely.

My ride to the hospital in Neville the next day was long. I was filled with remorse that the curse might somehow have caused the tragedy. When I arrived at Tef's hospital room, he was drinking water through a glass straw with clenched teeth. His jaw was broken. It seemed that casts covered every extremity. Those on his legs and arms were suspended by various ropes and pulleys.

Tef's eyes showed tears as he looked up at me. Because of the metal device inserted in his jaw, he had difficulty speaking. I had to lean in close to listen.

"Cezno . . . you know . . . how thick Stretch's neck was? How . . . could it have been broken like that? I'll never . . . understand."

"Listen, Tef, you'll get over this."

But he never did. Because of that single incident and his continued drinking, Teflon's great potential went down the drain. He became a hopeless drunk who happened to marry a schoolteacher kind enough to take care of him. Over the years in drunken stupors, he would call various fraternity brothers late at night, including me, to rant and rave about things that had happened long ago. Some years ago, I lost touch with him.

I often wondered whether Tef ever leaned about the curse. If so, did he conclude that I had caused the tragic collision? As discerning as he was, I felt certain that he had surmised that something like that had happened.

Chapter 19

At the time of her death, my favorite aunt, Bertha, had lived with us in Erie for many years. Her death was very painful for me. I'd gotten to know her well and considered her a close friend, although I never expected that she would make me sole beneficiary under her will.

I was astounded further when I discovered at the will reading that my legacy involved a considerable amount of money, a large portion of which I would later give to my parents to cover the "rent" they refused to assess against Bertha while she had lived with us. I was convinced that Bertha would have favored such a move, and the balance came at just the right time to cover the cost of law school.

Bertha's funeral took place in town, at Saint Stephen's Episcopal Church. As I listened to the slow, mournful throbbing of the organ, I got to thinking about Bertha. If she had been there, I know she would have hated the somber tone.

When visiting us during the holidays before her move-in, her mood was always upbeat. I'm remembering one Christmas in particular. Although she was always a ball of fire, on that occasion she exhibited an extra enthusiasm I hadn't seen. It was a Christmas the family would never forget, a real bamboozler.

As I was in my underwear in my room when Dad shouted up the stairs for me, I lost the opportunity to go downtown with him to pick up Bertha and bring her to our house for Christmas dinner. Some thirty minutes later, he returned.

"HAALLOOO," she bellowed as she entered. Mom stepped out of the kitchen to say hi, gave Bertha a kiss, and re-entered her domain.

"Hello there, Adrian," Bertha said.

"Hi, Aunt Bertha," I answered as I descended the stairs. She leaned in to kiss me on the cheek, and I noticed the smell of ginger and detected the faint rattling of her false teeth.

Our house was Christmas-ready. As always, a fully decorated Christmas tree stood in the corner of the dining room; as always, the smell of simmering turkey pervaded the downstairs; as always, my electric train was laid out under the tree, and Bruce, the family dog, with a large red bow on his collar, was predictably underfoot.

My overriding desire was to remove the itchy pants Mom had insisted I wear and replace them with jeans so that I could be comfortable playing with my trainset; but Mom and Dad had warned me that if I tried to make myself scarce, there would be "consequences." As a twelve-year-old, on several occasions I had learned what that term meant.

As I stood in the front hall beside Bertha, Dad appeared and kissed her cheek while holding out a glass of sherry. Aunt Bertha back then favored the kind of metal-rimmed eyeglasses that have become fashionable only recently. Tall and thin, she wore a gray blouse and a plain gray suit. Her hair, pulled back into a bun, was as gray as her blouse.

She appeared to be in her late sixties, but it was tough to tell. My dad, who was related to her, had no idea how old she was. Attractive as she was, Bertha had never married, but Dad was certain that a man had been living with her for the past several years. He also discovered that her paramour had died only recently. To avoid embarrassing her, he never let on that he knew about any of it.

When Dad offered a glass of sherry to holiday guests, it signaled that an exchange of conversation before supper would begin in the living room. Bertha, as usual, began telling us of people and places from the past we'd never heard of. Dad and I were struggling mightily to appear interested when Mom saved the day by calling us to dinner. The plan was to finish dinner and then retire to the living room to open presents while consuming our desserts.

I was anxious for the present-opening phase to begin and suffered silently through the meal. We had just seated ourselves in the living room after dinner when Bertha abruptly stood up. "This year, I have a special surprise for Dennis and Ida Mae," she said. "In fact, it is so special and exciting that I'd like to give it to them right off."

With that, she reached into her purse and pulled out a large envelope and handed it to Dad. Beside him on the couch, Mom watched intently as he opened it. Both gasped when they saw the contents: two first-class, round-trip tickets to Paris plus two-weeks' worth of accommodations at some fancy hotel whose name I don't remember and couldn't pronounce if I did.

Flabbergasted, Mom and Dad sat in stunned silence as the enormity of it all began to sink in. In prior years, the gifts had included books or sweaters or ties with nothing spent on either side more than twenty dollars.

My father finally broke the silence. "You're very kind, Bertha, but we can't accept this. Although a wonderful gesture, it's just too much. You can't afford it. No, we can't accept this."

With the last few words, his voice cracked. He was almost crying.

"Bertha, we thank you, but it's just too much," Mom said.

"Don't be silly," Bertha answered. "I want you both to have this."

"We just can't," Dad said.

"Now wait just a minute. If I didn't want you to have Paris, I wouldn't have given it to you. Besides, the tickets and hotel reservations are noncancelable. Who could I possibly get to go in your place?"

"Go yourself," my father answered, "with one of your lady friends. You'll have a ball."

"Oh, yes, wonderful—two old spinsters sitting beside the Eiffel Tower. No. Paris is for young people, like you. If you don't go, the reservations will go wanting; I can promise you that."

The conversation went back and forth in that manner for several minutes until Dad observed signs that Mom was weakening. I'd already picked up on them—a faraway look, accompanied by a faint smile. Not one to miss the obvious, Dad asked to be excused with Mom for a moment, and when they returned from the kitchen, I knew by looking at them that Bertha had won.

"We'll accept your generous offer on one condition and that is that you'll join us for dinner as soon as we get back," Dad said.

"Gladly. I love to come here. I always feel so comfortable and welcome."

Mom and Dad were smiling broadly when they got into the family car for the drive to the airport. I'd helped them by placing their suitcases in the car and had received a kiss on the cheek from each as a reward.

Two days later, a moving van led by a yellow cab showed up in front of our house. Soon, Bertha appeared at the front door with two movers. She told them to deposit her things in the empty room on the third floor.

At dinner that night, Bertha and I talked.

"Adrian, I know your mother and father will have a conniption when they discover that I've moved in."

"You're probably right about that, Aunt Bertha," I said with a smile.

"It may go easier if you were to support me. Do you want me to live here?"

"Sure I do. It's just that Mom had Granddaddy with us until he died two years ago at the age of ninety-six. She's not going to be too excited about starting all over again with someone new."

I continued, "And then Aunt Olga, my other grandfather's sister, wanted to move in while Granddaddy was still here. They said no to Olga, which was not too surprising."

Bertha looked up at me with a wry smile. "Did Aunt Olga ever send your parents to Paris?"

"Well, no."

"Adrian, I've got to tell you something."

I nodded.

"While your family is still around you, it seems like the good times will last forever."

I remained silent.

She continued, "But it doesn't. It doesn't last; believe me."

I'm not sure whether she wanted me to say something, so I continued to stay quiet.

"The time comes when everything changes. The people disappear or die. It's terrible to think about it now, but it'll happen to you."

I nodded.

"Adrian, there's nothing worse than being alone. There's no one to talk to. One day blends into the next. Loneliness begins to control everything." Tears were forming in her eyes. "How can I describe loneliness to you?" She paused. "What's the worst thing that has ever happened to you, so far?"

"When Christy died," I answered.

"Of course—your first dog. Well, imagine that pain, the pain you felt then, never ceasing. Imagine it as a constant, unremitting hurt. That's what loneliness feels like. What do you think about that?"

"I don't think I'd like it."

Right then, I was imagining the pain she described, knowing how lonely she must have been to cause her to conjure up her clever scheme. I hoped that she would pull it off. She was one neat lady.

Naturally, at the age of twelve I had no idea how to get in touch with my parents, so I didn't have to feel guilty about keeping them in the dark about Bertha's secret. The two weeks passed quickly. On the last day, I received a phone call telling me that Mom and Dad had arrived and were about to leave the airport. Soon after that, they were at the front door.

"Oh hi, Bertha," Dad said as he stepped in. "I didn't expect to see you here. Did the Kellys have a problem?" My parents had asked the Kellys to watch out for me in their absence. They lived across the street with a tribe of children, one of whom was my best friend. The plan was for me to live by myself with easy access to the Kellys for food and lodging and anything else I might need.

"The Kellys are fine," Bertha said.

I suggested to Dad that I help with the luggage. I was just prolonging the agony, but I had to do something to divert their attention until the time was right. Soon enough, Dad and Mom were in the living room regaling Bertha and me with stories of Paris, often evoking laughter.

Aunt Bertha held her expensive Limoges pillbox they gave her as if it was the most precious object on the face of the earth. Then she began to speak. I held my breath.

"I'm pleased, so pleased, that you enjoyed your trip. However, I've now got a confession to make," she said.

Sitting on the couch, Mom and Dad leaned forward, not knowing what to expect.

Bertha said, "My plan was to bribe you—with the trip, I

mean. You see, I'm devastated by the prospect of being alone indefinitely. I'd like to live here with you, in the extra room, the one upstairs. I won't be any trouble and I'll pay my way, just like a boarder, and help with the cooking and dish washing if you want me to."

"Well—," my father said.

Mom interrupted him. "We're flattered, but—"

Bertha then interrupted her. "You're still young. You don't know what it's like to be old and lonely with no idea about your future while watching all of the people you've known and loved move away or die."

"No, we don't, Bertha, but we will," Dad said. "Just like you, we've got our own future to be concerned about. Plus, we're forced to live very modestly because my company is notorious for its low pay. Even this house is an uncertainty. It's a rental and could be taken from us at any moment."

"I have money. I can help," Bertha answered.

"You'll need your money," Dad said. "You'll be facing potential medical problems that all of us must face as we get older. No, you'll need your money, and we'll need ours. Adrian will be entering college in a half a dozen years. I just wish I could afford to reimburse you for the cost of the trip. Under the circumstances, I feel that we've taken advantage of you."

"There's probably one more thing I should tell you," Bertha said.

"What's that?" my father asked.

"I've already moved in—my things are in the third-floor room at this moment and were placed there shortly after you two left for Paris."

Bingo! Bertha had just played her trump card.

At that point, I figured it was time for me to make my exit. I heard no response to Aunt Bertha's comment as I crossed the floor toward the stairs to the second floor, and all remained silent as I ascended. The deadening silence continued even as I opened the door and entered my bedroom.

As you might expect, Aunt Bertha won a second victory that day. She stayed with us until the day she died nine years later. During that entire time, she never went with us to Chautauqua, claiming that the family should have time alone during vacations. Unfortunately, she wasn't alive when I started law school, but she did attend my wedding the summer after I graduated from college. Dana, my new wife, adored her.

Chapter 20

Mom died of a stroke a few months before my law school graduation. Ida Mae was a wonderful woman sorely missed by all of us. Just as the dean was handing me my law degree, I somehow felt her beside me and choked up. Even though I don't believe in ghosts, when the sense of her presence hit me, I held up the line behind me for a few seconds as I gasped for air.

Dennis—what I had begun calling Dad after I'd reached a certain age—showed up for the graduation. His blond hair was turning gray, but he still cut a handsome figure. Mom had kept him thin and in shape and made it clear to women of all shapes and sizes that she adored him. She also made it clear that she would cut to pieces any one of them who tried to seduce him. I was pleased when she told me I was his spitting image.

At the time of her death, Mom had published three books of poetry, all well received. In her mind, this success was an anomaly because she always felt that West Virginia was not noted for producing gifted writers. Her influence upon me was evident in my love of poetry, but unlike her, I aspired to write verse with a humorous touch.

BUGGED

Imagine the stories
the grown-up aphids tell
to the little ones
with popping eyes,
the tiny sapsuckers
who haven't yet grown
to full size.

Let them plant an egg in you.
Then, you'll find out.
You'll become the host, they shout.
The egg will hatch
and you'll be devoured
from the inside out.
So, when you hear us yell
Wasp! Wasp! Wasp!
You've got to fly like hell.

One young blade had a question.

There's a hand up
in the back.

I want to tell you how I feel, he says.
You tell me that I'll become the host
for an attacking wasp
who plants an egg inside me that hatches
and makes me its meal?

The grown-ups all nod.

> *Who is it that makes these rules*
> *and where can I appeal?*

Amusing perhaps, but not destined for Wordsworthian greatness. Dennis never much liked my poetry. When I visited him on his deathbed, I hinted that I planned to read one of my poems at his memorial service, which prompted a loud guffaw. Thus restrained, when the time came, I sat silently in my seat. Nevertheless, I did say a silent prayer for Dennis and shed a few tears. I always loved him despite his obvious aversion to my poetry.

"Adrian," he would say, "stick to prose."

Chapter 21

It was raining so hard that the wipers, at high-speed, struggled to peel even a momentary opening. Inside the car, the defroster couldn't cut a hole in the fogged-over windshield.

Few cars were on the road. I had just passed the Ohio Eastern Toll Gate on my way to Cleveland from my home in the suburbs of Pittsburgh. The rhythmic pounding of the wipers and the sound of the rain on the roof heightened my depressed mood. I was remembering Dana's cancer diagnosis. How many years ago was that?

Doctor Allen had responded with predictable swiftness to Dana's symptoms—abdominal pain, a distended stomach, and vaginal bleeding—by calling us both to meet with him immediately. Too soon we were standing in front of a shadow box in his office.

"There it is," he said, pointing to a spot on the film. "It's about the size of an orange."

Dana and I leaned in close to look. Sure enough, the film showed an ugly, round object at the end of his finger.

"What does it mean, Doctor?" Dana asked.

"You've got to know it isn't good," he said. "The first step is to determine whether it's cancerous. Let's pray that it's benign. Whatever it turns out to be, though, they'll have to remove it surgically."

Unable to speak, I felt a cold fear possess me. Unbeknownst to both of us, the doctor had just given Dana a death sentence. It would not be fully carried out for eleven years thanks to a brilliant oncologist who would step in to help us. At the beginning of our marriage, I had no defense when I learned of drastic events affecting other people except to reason that they couldn't possibly happen to me because I'd been blessed by God and favored by the universe. I was forced to change that thinking radically in the upcoming weeks and months and years.

Today, the rain didn't let up. Although many cars had pulled over, I continued to push ahead, anxious to arrive at the hotel where the ABA Section of Litigation Annual Fall Meeting was being held. I expected to see one or more of my lawyer friends at the bar, and in my mind, I could taste and smell the first Southern Comfort Manhattan, a drink that Dennis had introduced me to when I turned eighteen. Still unable to see the road clearly, I was reluctant to wipe my hand across the inside windshield; from experience, I knew that it would cause a smear that would remain for days. As a compromise, I cranked up the defroster and reduced my speed.

Back when Dana was first seeing the doctor, my religion and my philosophy of life pretty much coincided. Spoiled as a child, I ended up wrongly thinking that the Fates somehow favored Dana and me. The remedy against all loss was simple. In Dana's case, if I just concentrated long enough on the tumor being benign, that's what it would be. All would be well. I believed then that I could sabotage the normal course of events by the sheer force of my will. The tumor could not be malignant, I thought, since Dana was still a young woman when it was discovered. That wouldn't be fair. But not only was the tumor malignant, the cancer was diagnosed as ovarian, one of the deadliest forms. The scene in my memory shifts. With Dana's blood still spattered on his white coat, Dr. Randall, Dr. Allen's teammate, came to see me in the tiny room where I was sitting after the first surgery.

"It went very well," he said as he entered. "She's doing fine." Pause. "Do you have any questions?"

"Will it come back?"

"We did our best to remove it all. You've got to understand, though, there are a lot of tiny spuds, almost invisible." He put his forefinger very close to his thumb. "Smaller than a speck, hard to see. It's almost impossible to remove them all. Just one left inside can bring it back."

"But you got them all. You got all the spuds, didn't you, Doctor?"

"The odds are that it will come back. It's the nature of the disease. If nothing happens in five years, she may make it. But that's doubtful."

He was correct. It came back in five years and six months. It came back however hard I tried to wish and pray it away.

The rain had not let up. From what I could see outside, it was as though I was the only person left on earth. The road was clear but sodden. I was back to thinking about the history of it all. I'm not sure when I first began to hear the voice, but it came to me on this day in full force.

There is no hope for a sexual relationship with your wife, sick as she is. Adrian, no one expects you to go without sex.

I tried to tune out the voice, but it continued, *Don't try to be a saint. You've got unmanageable urges. It's been years. No one expects you to get through this without many, many affairs.*

"Adultery. You want me to commit adultery—while my wife is dying of cancer? What kind of a brute do you think I am?"

The voice in my head continued, *There is a footnote to the commandment against adultery. It doesn't apply to someone who's experiencing what you've been going through. There're always exceptions.*

I elected to ignore the voice.

I was remembering again. The second surgery occurred on schedule. At that point, Dr. Randall was on a leave of absence and his young assistant, who called Dana "sweetie" because he couldn't remember her name, did the job. He declared right off that her condition was inoperable, causing him to sew her back up without doing anything further.

Afterward, Dana and I were convinced that this boorish young man was only looking for his fee, convinced as we were that the operation would not have been necessary if the proper tests had been run beforehand. This same doctor pronounced that Dana would not survive for more than three months (she lasted several years). Then, following the surgery that should never have taken place, she suffered a condition known as ARDS—acute respiratory distress syndrome—that necessitated her being placed on a respirator.

For the trip to Cleveland, I'd retained a nurse's aide to care for her. As the rain pounded on the windshield, I asked the same questions I had asked so many times before: *Why Dana? Why now?* But what I was really asking was *Why me?* Self-pity added to my sense of vulnerability. The voice seemed to know this. It came down on me at that moment.

How much can you take? You've been thrown into the valley and then dragged back out feet first. This is the time that you most need companionship. Dana can't give you that any longer.

"Think of what Dana has been through," I answered. "Besides, it's wrong, flat-out wrong. Don't you see that? I can't do it. I won't do it."

I found myself shouting.

In the intensive care unit, we watched the machine breathe for her with a whooshing sound as it attempted to refurbish her lungs. At the lowest point, she began to rally, faintly at first, and then with resonance and vigor.

I was remembering again in the car on the ride to Cleveland. The voice continued, *Adrian, you can't keep this up. You're being held hostage.*

A huge truck passed with its horn blaring. I eased up on the gas to give myself some distance. A mile or so up the road, somewhat obscured by the sheets of rain, I saw a car off to the side backed by a police car with its top light spinning. The brazen truck driver in front of me didn't even slow down as he passed. Old feelings of vulnerability and separation hit me as I studied the rain's relentless pattern. The voice in my head was at me again.

Go ahead. You've got her number. Use the phone in the rest area. No one will ever know.

I knew what the voice was referring to. It was talking about a telephone number—Margo's telephone number. I'd suppressed that information in the back of my mind. Casually, at a recent luncheon, a Chautauqua friend told me that Margo was now in Cleveland.

"Adrian, she's still a fox after all these years," he said.

I asked him if he had her number. He gave me one of his cards with her number written on it. The card was still with me, tucked away in my wallet. The rain continued. The incessant pounding of the wipers was the only constant. Then, the voice was at me again.

Go ahead; call her. I dare you.

I didn't answer. Instead, I stared straight ahead, thinking of Margo. I remembered the kiss by the lake behind the High School Club. The voice could sense an opening.

It's been so long. Don't you want to see what she looks like? Don't you want to talk to her? What harm could come of that?

In an instant, I was pulling into a rest stop. I grabbed several quarters out of the console between the seats and began walking toward the building in long-shot hopes of finding a phone there. I didn't want to use my cell phone—I didn't want to leave a trace of the call. As I walked, I told myself that I would talk to her briefly to see how she was doing and then hang up, nothing more.

Sure, sure. Of course, that's all you'll do, but you could ask her to meet you in the hotel bar, the voice said.

My excitement made my hands sweat. To my astonishment, in an age where payphones are rare, a lone phone hung on an outside wall. I made a conscious effort not to drop the receiver as I dialed Margo's number while I looked at her number on the card. The phone connected. I counted the rings—one, two, three.

A voice answered. It was Margo's.

"Hellooo."

Her voice was melodious, just as it had been so many years before.

"Hellooo," she said again.

Without answering, I hung up the receiver with a loud *bang*.

The voice in my head wasn't through.

What are you doing? You know you want to see her. You'd be with her at the hotel bar with easy access to your room upstairs.

As a final act of defiance, I tore the card with her number into pieces as I walked away from the phone toward my car.

Chapter 22

Recently, Dana noticed a swelling in her neck. She telephoned Sam McMasters, her oncologist, to advise him of this development, and he scheduled a morning appointment for the very next day. A few hours before the appointment, I came downstairs to find Dana dozing on the yellow settee in the sunroom, her favorite spot. She had dressed herself and was waiting for me to appear. These days, I slept upstairs in the master bedroom while she slept on a mechanical bed set up in the dining room downstairs.

I paused to study her. Over the eleven years she had suffered with ovarian cancer, her body hadn't held up well. Known for her spectacular beauty in college—perfect legs, incredible figure, regal bearing —now, because of the chemo, she'd taken on the gnarled appearance of an old woman. Yellow skin hung loosely on her bones. She was just one year older than me, and with her bad teeth, ragged skin, and sagging breasts, more than one nurse had misidentified her as my mother. The mistake always wounded her deeply.

As she dozed, I studied the marks—jagged gouges really—that remained embedded in her arms. When the veins gave out from chemo injections, the doctors rigged up a port to accommodate the lines. Likewise, when problems developed in her digestive tract, they added a colostomy bag, now hidden beneath her velour blouse. Looking down at her, I wondered why I could not feel sadness or sympathy or even anger. Instead, there was a numbness that had emerged after several years of caring for her. It wasn't that I didn't love her. No, it had to be something else.

Sam's office is in Oakland, a section of Pittsburgh where a significant number of the city's doctors and college professors could be found. The trip there would take approximately forty minutes, so we had a few minutes to relax before our departure.

Outside, it was a perfect fall day. Leaves of orange, red, and yellow showed colors that matched the lemons, tomatoes, and oranges Dana had placed on the windowsill.

Soon, the leaves will begin falling off the trees, I thought, *impetus for my fastidious neighbor to begin raking.*

Abruptly, Dana's eyes fluttered open, signaling her initial effort to remember where she was.

"Oh, it's you, Adrian. I thought I heard something. How are you doing?"

"Just dandy. I'm glad you had a chance to nap a bit."

Although we had had our differences over the years, I'd never gotten over her bravery after the cancer hit. Sometimes, her eyes would puddle up, presumably at the thought of never seeing her grandchildren—we had three kids—but those moments were rare. Only recently did her cancer fears take over. The sudden swelling in her neck triggered a reaction somewhere between frenzy and full panic.

"We'd better get going. We don't want to keep the doctor waiting," I said.

"You know what this is all about, don't you?"

"I think so."

"Sam's going to tell us that the swelling means that the

cancer's now in my bloodstream. He's also going to say that it's just a matter of time, probably a few months, after telling us that there's nothing more he can do for me since the time for chemo has passed."

As usual, she waited for some display of emotion from me. I showed none. Instead, in silence I began to lift her from the settee knowing that a battle against Dana's instincts would be, as always, futile. Even so, I wasn't sure I agreed with the prognosis. The disease had dragged on for so long, there didn't seem to be any reason to expect a radical change.

"Well, let's not jump the gun on this. Let's wait to hear what Sam has to say," I said.

"I'm telling you what Sam will say." Irritation marked her voice.

Dana's wheelchair was already packed in the car trunk, so it was just a matter of assisting her across the porch and into the garage. Because of her drop foot, the going wasn't easy. I had to support most of her weight the entire way. Then, I eased her onto the front seat and helped her buckle up.

I turned the car around in our driveway and proceeded along West Waldheim Road. Fox Chapel gave us the opportunity to live in a peaceful, rustic setting, equidistant from Oakland and downtown Pittsburgh. Oversized yards and well-tended gardens complemented each stately structure.

"What's happening in the news?" I asked.

I often asked her this question when I wanted to hide behind conversation. Even as battered as she was from the disease, her mind was as keen as ever. She'd become so fast with crossword puzzles that most had become boring. Bridge had begun to arouse a similar reaction in the months before she became too sick to play. Meanwhile, she'd gotten so good at Jeopardy that I listened with amazement each time she snapped out the answers.

To fill the void caused by her lost pursuits, she became a news junkie of sorts with a special preference for the *New York Times*.

Her strategy was simple: If she couldn't participate directly in world events, she would participate indirectly through news sources. The news provided us many opportunities to talk about everything but her health.

This morning, Dana wasn't falling for my ploy to avoid any meaningful conversation, however. "You really can't face up to it, can you?" she said.

"Face up to what?"

"What Sam is going to tell us."

I didn't answer. Having crossed the Highland Park Bridge, we proceeded up Washington Boulevard. I glanced at the abandoned structure that once had housed an Eat'n Park restaurant, now boarded up and desolate, wondering why such relics became noteworthy in Pittsburgh when they were commonplace in so many other cities.

"What're you thinking?" Dana asked.

"I'm thinking about what Sam's going to say."

"I've already told you what he's going to say. You never listen to me. You're trapped in a dream world. It's time you grew up."

I didn't answer. Knowing that she was correct about my inability to express myself to her, I didn't want to spar. Besides, I had no counterargument to rebut the immaturity label.

Still on Washington Boulevard, I stopped at the light at Frankstown Boulevard. Looking over at Dana, I saw that she was doing that thing she did with her thumbs as she stared straight ahead. Above her clasped hands vigorous twiddling was in progress—first one thumb on top, then the other. After the second surgery, it was a practice she resorted to often.

As the light changed, I stepped on the gas. We were now on Fifth Avenue. At the traffic light at Fifth and Highland, I again looked over at her. Still twiddling.

"We should talk about what'll happen after my death."

"It's too early in the morning for that."

"You always have some excuse. Now's the time, not later."

She reminded me, once again, that her assets consisted primarily of money that her mother and father had given her over the years. She added that under her will, she had left all of it to me with the understanding that I would transfer whatever was left to the children after covering medical expenses.

"Knowing how much you love the children, I'm willing to trust you to do that."

She was correct. I loved the children openly and without reservation.

Dana paused before beginning again. "It certainly did not end up the way we'd planned. I have a disease that has made me old and ugly. It's no wonder you no longer love me."

I hated these pronouncements. She was forcing me to express feelings that I had difficulty sharing. Nevertheless, I attempted to give her an answer.

"I do love you," I said and looked over at her and smiled. "And I wouldn't worry too much about what you look like; you're still the same person underneath."

"We should talk about your next wife."

"*What?*"

"We should talk about your next wife."

"Are you serious?"

"I'm completely serious."

"What makes you think I'll remarry?"

"I know you. You adore women. And I've been thinking about who it should be."

"Oh, you have. And what have you decided?"

"We're almost at Sam's office now. We'll talk about it later."

On Aiken Avenue, I turned toward an office building adjacent to the University of Pittsburgh Medical Center and into a garage located below Sam's office. After I parked, Dana studied herself in the vanity mirror while applying lipstick.

"How can you love anything as ghastly as I am?"

"You let me worry about that. If you insist on knowing, let me tell you that your appearance now is only confirmation of how beautiful you were then. Anyone else would look like the Wicked Witch of the West by now. You don't."

Unsmiling, she continued to look in the mirror. Recently, a twitching at the corner of her mouth had begun. It was there now when she turned to look at me.

I continued, "As I said before, you are the same person you were when all of this began, in spite of everything, and that's what's most important."

She could see through such fawning comments with ease.

We were on the elevator on the way up to Sam's office. Through all of it, Sam had supervised her progress perfectly, giving her chemo at times when it seemed most appropriate. Despite his best efforts, the tumor returned and kept enlarging.

"I've always tried to be honest with you folks," Sam said when we were seated in front of him.

"That you have, Sam," I answered.

"This lump in your neck is very serious, Dana. It shows that the cancer is in your bloodstream. There's nothing more I can do for you."

"I know, Sam, I know," she said.

Dana adored Sam. I could hear the pain in her voice and his. Tears were beginning to well up in Dana's eyes. I knew she was thinking of the children

"Doctor, what'll happen now?" I asked.

"It may be three months or five months, but eventually the tumor, as it enlarges, will poison her. It'll be a quiet death. She'll just fall off to sleep."

"What about more chemo?" I asked.

"It's too late for that now, Adrian. I'm sorry."

"You shouldn't be," I said. "Not at all. You've done everything in your power to help her. Patients with ovarian cancer usually last three to five years at most. You have kept Dana alive for eleven. It's a miracle. You walk on water."

There was nothing more to say.

On the way home, Dana didn't want to talk. Eventually, she asked me to buy her a half-gallon bottle of gin, which I did on a stop at the liquor store. I knew what was coming, but there was nothing I could do to stop it. I referred to it as the *black rage* that exploded every time she had too much to drink and sometimes when she had not touched a drop.

As we drove up the hill to our house, she looked over at me.

"We've got to talk about your next wife," she said.

"I don't want to talk about that."

She seemed to be content with that answer.

She died in three months as Sam had predicted. In all that time, the subject of my remarriage never came up again.

Chapter 23

At a young age, I learned about Bridget's prophecy that I would be involved in a murder. Over the years, it caused me a great deal of anxiety. The uncanny part? What she said was dead-on. Her prophecy came to pass.

The incident came about shortly after Dana's death. I was practicing law in the Remington law firm in Pittsburgh at the time. Brad Wilson headed the litigation section. He hated my guts, so I was reluctant to visit his office for any reason. One day, I hesitantly knocked on his door and poked my head in. He was sitting at a huge desk, no papers on it in sight, that dwarfed him. As I entered, I thought of the maxim that a cluttered desk signified a cluttered mind and chuckled to myself as I speculated what an empty desk might mean.

He bellowed me in and remained seated. Like Andrew Jackson, his most prominent feature was his white mane. The change to white had occurred quite suddenly when he was still in his forties, making the lawyers speculate about what might have caused it.

"Close the door," he said.

He had a strange way of speaking, as though he had a speech impediment. I joked with one litigator that it was like he'd used

Demosthenes's technique to improve his speaking ability but forgot to remove the pebbles.

"Have a seat. What's up?"

I sat down, then paused for effect. "I'll get right to it," I said. "Brad, I'm burned out."

"How so?"

"I've tried three cases in a row—"

"How'd you do?"

"Lost all three." He well knew this.

"Bummer."

As always, his wrinkled sportscoat was hanging over the back of one of his chairs. The tie, persistently red, was partially pulled down. The eyes, close-set, were a colorless gray. I never heard anyone describe him as having a great profile, but what he lacked in looks, he tried to replace with tall tales about his litigation prowess. He was always bragging that he'd never lost a case, a position that I found quite implausible. Even if true, I was certain that the result had come about because of successful screening of cases or from early settlements rather than courtroom excellence. As section head, he got the initial shot at picking the winners. I suspect that any cases that appeared to be losers he delegated immediately to other lawyers in the firm, like me.

I continued, "I need some time off."

"Do you have any vacation time left?"

"No. That's why I'm here."

"Take two weeks."

"Many thanks."

I wasted no time in getting out of there. Although I was reluctant to ask for anything from him, I'd crawl over hot coals for a few extra days of vacation. He'd just given me two weeks, but he'd done it with the air of the head of the manor bestowing largesse upon a peasant.

The first week in Cancún was rather uneventful. I visited

some ruins and drank a lot of piña coladas by the pool. In the second week, things perked up significantly. A young woman by the name of Judy appeared. I noticed her right off. A bartender named Joe was working the thatched hut that day.

"Hey, Mr. Spencer, this lovely lady is also from Pennsylvania," Joe said.

She was at the far end of the bar. I moved to the stool beside her.

"What part of Pennsylvania?" I asked.

"Philadelphia. How about you?"

"Beautiful Pittsburgh."

"Good town."

"What do you do?"

"Paralegal."

"What firm?"

"Duggan, Hennessy."

"A big one." I took a swig of my drink, trying to be casual. "Did you ever hear of the Remington firm in Pittsburgh?"

"Of course. One of the big two or three. I applied there. Got turned down."

"Bummer." Another sip. "What's your name?"

"Judy Sternhagen."

"I'm Adrian."

By then, I'd had a chance to take a good look. She was very attractive. Her shiny black hair was pulled back. She had long perfect legs accentuated by a black bathing suit over which she wore a linen blouse that did its best to contain her figure. I put her age in the mid-twenties.

At first, I thought she'd have no interest in an out-of-shape widower. Despite my obvious paunch, bits of gray hair, and baggy swimming trunks, she quickly refuted my first impression. When she removed her sunglasses to reveal a beautiful pair of brown eyes, I began to think that the second week in Cancún might not be so bad.

We had dinner the first night. All went well. Casual conversation prevailed. Didn't try to kiss her outside her door, although I knew I was weakening. At dinner the second night, she asked me to share my history.

"I've told you about me. What about you?" she asked.

"Well, first off, I'm a widower. My wife died of cancer a few months ago."

"I'm so sorry. We have that in common. My husband died two years ago."

"Sorry to hear that. Was he a cancer victim?

"No, it was suicide . . . a long story."

I elected not to press for details.

"I'm a litigator," I said. "I'm down here for some R&R. Got my ass kicked in the last three cases."

"That's too bad." Suddenly, she reached across the table to grab my hand. "Adrian, I'm afraid something terrible is going to happen to me."

"What the hell are you talking about?"

"I came down here to think about my course of action. They can't take the chance I'll make the wrong decision."

"Who's *they*?"

"The law firm . . . one lousy bastard is leading the charge."

"Who's that?"

"Strike Brenner. He's ruthless, totally untrustworthy. Unfortunately, he's the managing partner. His evil seeps down the food chain to infect many of the young lawyers in the firm, particularly the newest associates."

"Why is he giving you a hard time?"

"He can't take the chance that I might turn on him. He suspects that I'll report him to the bar association. This time he'll be disbarred, for sure."

"You mean he's been in trouble before?"

"Yes."

"Sounds like a great guy."

"It gets worse. He drove my husband to suicide. Sam was a partner in the firm. I was a paralegal. Sam got on the wrong side of Brenner on some trivial matter. Brenner waited an appropriate amount of time and then took revenge. Took all of Sam's cases away. Then, he shut down the referrals. After that, he badmouthed Sam to firm clients. In a final step, after taking Sam's business away, he fired him, supposedly because of his lack of business. The humiliation was too much for Sam. Two years ago, he shot himself."

"This Brenner sounds like a real asshole."

"You don't want to know him. He destroys people just to show his power."

"And you're convinced he's after you?"

"Right. There's too much at stake. He won't do it himself. He'll hire someone. At first, I thought it might be you."

"I'm glad you've concluded otherwise."

"So am I." She smiled.

"I can see that you're itching to tell me the full story, so take a deep breath and let it all out."

She didn't hold back. She told me that her firm had been handling a case for a national pharmaceutical company involving billions in potential liability. It sounded like every defense firm's dream: a case where there is so much at stake the client is willing to throw vast amounts of money at it, including the kitchen sink. The fees don't matter. In litigation parlance, a case like that is a "ballbuster." An oversized group of class action plaintiffs had come together to file a suit. Their lawyers were led by a lawyer out of New York City by the name of Meridian Garfinkle, one of the best class action lawyers in the country. He and the other lawyers involved had committed a vast number of resources to the lawsuit.

She began to whisper as she leaned in closer.

"Realizing that this case would provide a gravy train for many years to come, Brenner assigned most of the firm's internal manpower to the defense while he took the billing credit. I was one of ten paralegals assigned. The firm also hired a profusion of expert witnesses to assist. His mistake was in keeping me on after Sam's suicide. I expect that he intended to seduce me as he has done with several other paralegals."

"What you're saying is that Brenner's firm has pulled out all the stops. If the case were to suddenly disappear, the result would be catastrophic."

"Correct."

"And they're convinced that you're prepared to deliver the *coup de grace*."

"Right again. Do you remember the product liability suit some years ago involving the exploding gas tanks?" she asked.

"Sure. Millions of automobiles were involved. It was a major class action."

"That's the one. You'll recall that the plaintiffs in discovery found an extremely damaging document."

"I have a vague recollection."

"The document proved that the car company was aware that the gas tanks could explode on impact. One company engineer concluded in a memo that it would be cheaper to settle the lawsuits than—"

"You mean—"

"Yes. The engineer's memo set forth that it would be cheaper to pay off future plaintiffs than to fix the defect in millions of cars. *Let 'em burn*—at least that's what the plaintiffs argued after they found the memo that gave that advice."

"How horrible. Let me guess. You found a document equally as damaging in the pharmaceutical case?"

"Bingo! One of the scientists in the company lab concluded in a memo that the prescription drug in question would kill thousands. Still, the company moved ahead to market it because the firm needed the revenue. Correction of the problem would be too costly."

"Incredible. When you discovered the document, what did you do?"

"Well, I showed it to Strike Brenner . . . right away."

"And what did he do?"

"He told me he'd keep the document in the safe in his office. He told me to burn all other copies."

"Did you do that?" I asked.

"What do you think?"

She smiled at me. Then, she said, "You're aware of the procedure in these cases?"

"Of course. First, each side gathers its own internal documents. Second, a team of paralegals and lawyers goes through the documents that are to be produced to see if any of the documents are damaging. Third, the documents are produced. Then, endless depositions are undertaken and years later the trial commences . . . if it gets that far. Most of these cases settle, especially when a crucial document is found, like the one you've described."

"Yes, and Strike Brenner can't risk that. The gravy train would shut down."

"I get the picture."

"I watched the first production closely. I wanted to see if the key document would be included."

"Was it?" I asked.

"Of course not. The company turned over thousands and thousands of documents, but not the key one."

"Big surprise! What did you do?"

"Well, I went to see Strike Brenner. He denied ever seeing such a document. Then, when I pressed him, he admitted he'd seen it but that it had been destroyed. At that point, he began threatening me. He said that if I didn't keep silent and play along,

I'd bring down the client as well as the firm. According to him, thousands of jobs were at stake. Then, he assured me that if I brought it up again, I'd be fired."

"Go on."

"That's when I decided to come down here—to think it over."

"We've got a real potboiler here. If it were a novel, it would be a bestseller," I said.

She smiled.

On the one hand, I wanted to help her. On the other hand, I became concerned that I might become the next target if what she told me was the truth and not part of an overactive imagination. Looking around the restaurant, I imagined that every male patron eating alone in the place was a hit man.

She said, "I've got two options. One is to forget the whole thing. The second is to turn the bastard in." She paused for a breath. "I've decided to go to the Disciplinary Board of the Pennsylvania Bar Association. I'm also planning to call on Mr. Garfinkle personally in New York."

"He's the lead lawyer for the class action plaintiffs?"

"Yes."

"Judy, you're a brave lady. I admire your honesty as well as your guts. But you're dealing with some very powerful people here. If you bring the document to light, you'll probably never work in a law firm again."

"I realize that, but I've got to do what's right. I'll find something else to do." She paused. "Listen. If anything happens to me, I've got several copies of the document hidden in my condominium in Philadelphia. They're in a small leather satchel behind the exhaust fan in my kitchen. Here's the address and an extra key."

"Judy, believe me, nothing's going to happen to you. This isn't a Hollywood movie."

I was wrong. Dead wrong. The next day, she disappeared. The police concluded that foul play most likely had been involved and speculated that it had occurred in the early morning as she was jogging along a path beside the ocean. They found her tennis shoe, nothing more.

According to the local police, the absence of a body wasn't surprising. Bodies in Cancún, they said, have a way of floating out to sea where they're never seen again, thanks to the sharks. I was never really a suspect, considering that I was having breakfast at the time Judy went missing. (I was never a jogger, and I never miss breakfast.) Two weeks later, there was still no sign of her. By then, I was back in Pittsburgh.

I waited a day or two and then drove to Philadelphia. The papers were right where she said they'd be. That day, I followed the course of action Judy had proposed. Still, I didn't want to do anything that would have such huge implications for the legal community without talking to someone in my own firm. As much as I hated to admit it, Brad Wilson was that person.

Prior to going to Wilson's office, I'd given him a brief description of what was involved. When I got there, Palmer, the managing partner, and Summerville, his second in command, were also present. I wasn't pleased, but I wasn't surprised. Palmer was a weasel, and Summerville was a Harvard-educated idiot.

Summerville, Wilson, and Palmer were lawyers who flourished in an atmosphere of controversy and politics. For them, there was only one rule: Play ball our way, or suffer the consequences. Summerville claimed to be a trial lawyer, but he hadn't tried a case in all the years I'd been with the firm. He'd been a judge until he discovered that he couldn't educate his children on a judge's salary. Soon after that, he came to the firm to receive a high salary that came with being a yes-man for Palmer.

"Ah, Adrian, have a seat," Wilson said.

I sat down.

"I've asked Julius Summerville and Perry Palmer to join us."

"I see that."

"Hope you don't mind, Adrian," Palmer said.

"Not at all. It's good to see you all," I lied.

"Adrian, we'll not beat around the bush. Brad has given us the facts. You're juggling a hot potato here. The document the paralegal found will have a tremendous impact. All three of us think you should bury it," Summerville said.

"Are you kidding? A young woman lost her life to preserve that document."

"You don't know what happened to her. It could just as easily have been a local serial killer. Maybe she went jogging in the wrong part of town, or maybe she'll turn up," Palmer said.

"I see you've done your homework."

Summerville went next. "All right, I'll get right to it. We get referrals from Strike Brenner's firm every year—several million dollars' worth. What's more, I went to Harvard with Strike. He's a close friend. We don't want to see him disbarred, and we don't want to see his firm go under."

"Let me see if I understand what's happening here," I said. "You want me to bury a document that is of critical importance in a lawsuit, and you want me to do it because otherwise our firm's finances might be adversely affected. And you want me to ignore the fact that a brave young lady probably died to preserve it."

It was Palmer's turn next. "Look, you've always been a troublemaker here, a real thorn in our side. If you don't play ball on this, you'll be fired."

"I get it. You're threatening to fire me unless I perform an illegal act?"

"Damn straight we'll fire you," Porter said.

The room went suddenly silent. No one spoke. Then, I stood up.

"Gentlemen, I've got a three-word response for you." I paused for dramatic effect. "Go to hell."

And that was it. I walked out the door.

Within a week, I'd given the document to the Disciplinary

Board of the Pennsylvania Bar Association. In the week following, I delivered a copy personally to Meridian Garfinkle, the lead lawyer in the class action lawsuit. The repercussions were as I'd expected. Not only was I fired from the Remington firm, but I was banished from the practice of law altogether. In the view of the legal community, I'd been a squealer, a whistleblower. And that couldn't be tolerated.

As it turned out, Strike Brenner's firm did survive (just barely), but he didn't—not as a lawyer anyway. The plaintiffs in the class action lawsuit cleaned up.

Judy's body was never recovered. Consequently, her family suffered greatly. Without a body, they couldn't bring any sort of legal action against Brenner. His disbarment brought them some peace of mind, though—that and the divorce he suffered soon after.

For the past two years, I've been spending my time as a writer—an unpublished one, unfortunately. I've been living in a small apartment in Pittsburgh, existing on meager savings.

I should add that I've never been happier in my life.

Judy, wherever you are, I hope you're proud of me.

Chapter 24

After some years, a strong job offer came my way—the slot of in-house counsel for a business called Monardo Construction Company. The opportunity came at the right time. By then, I was bored of writing unpublished prose and poetry.

Dominic Monardo wasn't the type to be moved to any extent by negative gossip, especially gossip from or about lawyers. When I described my history, he was most sympathetic and promised to disregard any negative comments from outside sources, especially lawyers, insisting instead that I deserved a medal for what I'd done. He made it clear that he didn't like lawyers but would make an exception in my case but only in my case.

When he told me to report for work the day following the initial interview, I was overjoyed.

"Adrian, you've got the job, but don't start looking around for someone to sue." He laughed.

"Boss, I'll be as calm and reserved as a clam," I answered.

I was excited to have a job—any job. Gone was the stigma of unemployment that had impeded any dating prospects following Dana's death and my departure from a large local law firm. Before that, prospective female candidates didn't like to hear that

I was living alone in an apartment just writing prose and poetry.

But my new position changed everything.

I noticed Heather right away at a church function. She was close to my age, had shiny blond hair, a good figure, a bright smile, and no ring on her finger. With unrestrained exuberance, she was distributing what she described as "holy meatballs" on a tray in the parish hall, where most of the social functions at Sunnyside Presbyterian Church took place.

This occasion was a coffee hour following the main service. The large room with basketball rims at each end easily accommodated several hundred parishioners. Offering her wares to the attendees, she stood at the center of the floor between hoops, so to speak. After a few brief pleasantries, I asked her a direct question.

"So, what's your story?"

She gave me appropriate details—married at eighteen, divorced seven years later, married a second time, divorced six years later, recently arrived in Pittsburgh, where her grandchildren were living, and had become a new member of Sunnyside.

At some point in the conversation, I gave her my personal story—widower, retired trial attorney, local resident, and a long-term member of the church. I was intrigued enough to ask for her phone number. When I called her the next day to ask her to dinner, she suggested Atria's in Aspinwall and asked permission to bring her three grandchildren.

Heather and the children were waiting for me in front of the restaurant when I arrived. She introduced me to Chloe, Plum, and Fiona. All three little girls were adorable. Like Heather, each had a crop of shiny golden hair. I soon became known as "Captain Adrian." Our date was going so well that after dinner I suggested that I bring the girls with me in my car. It was far roomier than Heather's, which had one of the girls' massive school projects in the back, making for a cramped ride. Heather agreed and helped me strap the girls in.

As I had never been to her house, the plan was for me to follow her there. Somehow, our cars got separated. Even though I had only a vague notion of where Heather lived, I took a chance to find her house on my own, thinking that the girls could help me when we got close. With all three in the backseat, I traveled out to Middle Road, where I stopped for directions at a country store. After several minutes inside, I returned to the car to find Plum sobbing.

"I thought it was a trap," she blurted.

Hearing my assurances that I had no bad intentions, Plum brightened up a bit. After one or two unsuccessful passes down a road where Heather supposedly lived, I concluded that the best bet was to go back to my residence so that I could call her on my cell phone, which, of course, I'd neglected to bring with me. By then, significant time had passed. I pulled into the parking lot next to my apartment house and noticed a police cruiser with an officer sitting inside. As I slid into my spot, he stepped out.

I spoke first. "You wouldn't happen to be looking for three little girls, would you?"

"Why, yes. Their grandmother called us," he said.

"Here they are, Officer," I said.

"Hmm," he said, looking at the girls. "Open the car, and let them out. They'll sit in the back of the cruiser," he said, pointing.

When they were safely inside, I looked at the three faces smiling up at me through the side window and wondered if they had ever been in a police car.

ADRIAN SPENCER, CHILD MOLESTER!

That was the headline I imagined. Not a pleasant thought. As a pedophile, I'd have to register with a local police station every time I moved. I'd always been noted for my rapport with children, but now that image would shift a bit.

"Where is she?" I asked.

"You mean the grandmother?" the officer asked.

"Yes, I mean the grandmother," I said through clenched teeth. "She should arrive shortly."

During the five or ten minutes that ensued, I seethed. No way was I ever going to date Heather again. She'd blown it and when she arrived, she looked a bit sheepish, which was some consolation, but not enough.

"You pegged me as a child molester," I told her.

"Oh, no, not at all. I never thought that. Not for a minute."

The police officer, standing to one side, was listening. But for a nearby streetlight and the inside light of the police car, the parking lot was pitch-dark. Still, there was enough light to see the strain on Heather's face.

"Look, why don't you come to my house with me and the girls. You've never seen it. I'll drive you there and back."

I didn't hesitate. "No thanks. I'm not in the mood. But thanks for a wonderful evening." With that, I turned dramatically on my heel and walked toward the apartment house. As far as I was concerned, Heather was history.

Destiny had other plans.

Heather called the next morning. "I'm soooo sorry." Her voice dripped with sincerity.

"You damn well ought to be. Did you think me capable of harming those little girls?"

"Of course not."

And so on.

I began to weaken. It was my daughter, Linda, who turned the tide for me. Living in Annapolis, she offered her advice over the telephone. "Dad, she hardly knew you. You drove off with her grandchildren. I'd have done the same thing."

"You'd have called the police?"

"Absolutely."

Thanks to my daughter, it wasn't long before Heather and I began dating seriously. Some weeks later, I ran into the police officer who was present that night. He smiled at me and waved as he stepped out of his cruiser.

"You were great," he said. "I'll never forget what you said to her when she asked you to come home with her: 'No thanks. I'm not in the mood. But thanks for a wonderful evening.'"

He laughed heartily. I smiled back at him.

"Are you still dating her?" he asked.

"Yes."

"No kidding?"

There was a note of disbelief in his voice.

Heather was an insurance adjuster with one of the big companies. When she was transferred to Atlanta, we both recognized that our relationship had no future. She said that she loved me but wasn't *in* love with me, which caused a struggle with romantic semantics that I've had trouble with ever since. Fortunately, I was able to follow biblical teachings, shaking Heather's "dust off my shoes" before moving on to the next candidate. Eventually, some friends fixed me up with someone who lived in Sewickley, a borough a short distance outside of Pittsburgh. I married Sara, the light of my life.

Chapter 25

Sara and I eventually moved to Shepherdstown, West Virginia, because her son, Sean, born during her first marriage, lived there with his family. He had become a pilot for one of the airlines assigned to Dulles Airport in Washington, DC. The commute to the airport was a little under two hours, which encouraged him to live in Shepherdstown.

Almost immediately, Sara and I became members of a local church. With her help, I confirmed my faith in God. In truth, years before I had first experienced a rekindling of my faith when an invisible presence woke me up as I was heading for an inevitable car crash. I didn't fail to see God's hand in my rescue.

Accordingly, I was ready to experience the bolstering of my faith that Sara helped me accomplish. Even so, we were ill prepared to deal with the difficult questions that she and I were encountering—*Is there a heaven?*, *Is it available to everyone?*, *Did God create the universe?*—to name just a few.

The last question was particularly vexing. Modern science has added gobs of new information that has gone well beyond our level of understanding, such as the Big Bang Theory, which left us wondering what existed before the Big Bang; notification that the universe is expanding, which left us wondering where it is going; and introduction to black holes, which left us wondering what was at the bottom.

And what about the discovery that the universe was created twelve billion years ago and the Earth about four billion years ago? Do we believe that God was around that many years ago to do the creating? My newly strengthened faith didn't help me come up with any helpful answers, and I began to wonder whether others were experiencing the same frustration. Have we come to know so much in the modern era that it's impossible to include God in the mix?

In time, I concluded that my faith could be affirmed if I applied the right formula. Certainly, I cannot speak for others, but in my own case, I decided that the only formula that would work occurred after discarding any attempt to make sense of it all. Since the difficult questions could never be resolved, why even try?

As a frustrated poet, I have attempted to use poetry to express those thoughts.

STUTTER STEPS

> Pastor, you say that God created the universe.
> Come on! That myth is for ignorant souls
> who don't have a clue.
> Since then, we've learned so much—
> billions of galaxies, containing billions of stars,
> along with bottomless black holes
> that are difficult to view,
> and planets, so many planets,
> many of which may be
> in galaxies like our own
> rotating around a single star.
> Since we don't even know

where the universe begins or ends,
isn't the concept of a God-created universe
a stretch too far?

Zelda, the gaps in our knowledge
shouldn't cause defeat.
We may be unable to calculate
the total number of stars
or to fashion a theory that tells us
what it's all about.
Still, isn't it just as easy
to admit our failings
as it is to doubt?

Pastor, you talk about faith—
precision, design, science, physics,
and mathematics are the only tools
that can bolster our faith.
The *faith* you describe is only for fools.

Zelda, the Bible tells us
to embrace our faith with zest,
like little children
who have no need
to apply any sort of a test.

Did you ever watch a young swimmer
standing at the edge of a pool
with his back to the water
and his arms crossed in front?
Looking straight ahead, he falls back,
letting the water embrace him
unconcerned about

> the formula for water
> or the reason it holds him up.
> Without looking back, he gives a shout
> confident that a safe landing
> will never be in doubt.
> Zelda, when you think about it,
> isn't that what faith is all about?

Once I discontinued my vain attempt to make sense out of everything, only then did my personal innermost faith come to the fore. From that point, there were no garbled theories to gum up my thinking. I came to know of God's existence because I could feel his presence in my heart. Call it the Holy Spirit or some cosmic interconnection if you will, but for me the feeling came to be there, and it was quite comforting.

How did it get there? That is the million dollar question. In my case, it was a simple matter of asking Jesus Christ to come into my life. Thereafter, there came countless instances when I was able to confirm that He remained there.

Chapter 26

Sara and I rented a cottage for a week at a place called Wahmeda, a vacation spot next to Chautauqua Institution. The rents were much more reasonable there and access to the Institution was readily available through a back gate. Soon after we arrived, I took her on a tour of the grounds. Bestor Plaza was just as it had been except that the famous fountain no longer attracted the teenage groups that had once inhabited assigned places on each of its four sides.

I told Sara about Margo and her aversion to rats. She laughed and asked me whether I'd dated her during subsequent summers, and I was at a loss to relate further details about Margo's present whereabouts. I suspected that her family had given up their cottage in favor of another vacation spot, but I had no idea what the choice might have been.

"Margo was beautiful but very impetuous, almost like a colt newly born."

"Do you have any clue what happened to her?"

"None. The only thing I know is that she failed to return the next summer." (I elected not to tell her about the close call on the way to Cleveland.)

"I suppose that her absence really crushed you."

I could sense a twinge of jealousy, so I changed the subject. "The Amphitheater is just ahead."

I told her about its availability at no charge before the board of directors got wise to the fact that people would willingly pay to hear the concerts and other entertainment events available there. It was the ideal place to listen to an orchestra because it was open on all sides, which permitted warm breezes to waft in from the lake. I told her about some of the great performances.

"The Kingston Trio performed there to a full-capacity audience."

"Were you there?"

"You bet. My age group went wild and when the songs kept coming, the old people got even louder. 'Scotch and Soda,' when they sang it, brought the house down."

"Did you take Margo?"

"No. That concert occurred several years after my Margo experience."

We proceeded down the road beside the Athenaeum Hotel, a huge Victorian structure facing Chautauqua Lake. It stood like a grand old lady proud of her verandas and balconies and wooden flourishes, all attributable to the architecture of an era long since out of style. As we approached, the hotel guests having lunch on the veranda nodded to us.

When we passed the High School Club, I noticed that the permanent bench Margo and I had sat on during the Fourth of July festivities was still there, but I refrained from describing the romantic interlude to Sara. I was concerned that she might become upset about it.

We were on the way to the Chautauqua Yacht Club to enjoy a sailing lesson on our anniversary. After a brief training session, we were assigned to one of the sailboats tied up on the long dock in front of the club.

"Are we able to sail the boat unsupervised?" Sara asked.

"Apparently so, but don't worry, I've sailed on this lake before." I was thinking of my experience during one or two sailing races, but then I remembered that I was only a lowly crew member, never a helmsman.

We sailed at a casual pace toward the famous Bell Tower, a brick structure containing a carillon of at least four bells that chimed out the hours and quarter hours.

"We better start sailing back. Would you like to take the helm?" I asked.

"You bet," she answered.

For several minutes, we proceeded without incident until Sara asked a crucial question. "Is the tiller supposed to do this?" She held it up in the air.

I'll not give the gory description of what happened after that except to confirm that we lived to sail another day.

Author's Note

Yes, *Passage to Chautauqua* is packed with snippets that come directly from my life. The character of Heather was inspired by a real person. An adolescent Margo did ask me to walk her home. The Boys and Girls Club, the Bell Tower, Bestor Plaza, and other Chautauqua landmarks have the same look today as they did then.

The narrative gives an accurate account of my first wife's cancer experience from first diagnosis onward. Diane (identified as Dana) appeared in my Milton class and came to Pittsburgh as my wife to reside in two separate suburbs (Shaler and Fox Chapel), both located near Highland Park where I grew up. The various descriptions of those areas are fairly accurate.

As a widower, I married Shannon Craig (identified as Sara) and lived with her in Sewickley (adjacent to Pittsburgh) before moving to Shepherdstown, West Virginia, in 2012 to be close to her son John (identified as Sean) and his family. John has been a United Airlines pilot for several years.

Delphic College was an imaginary substitute for Denison University in Granville, Ohio. Teflon will go nameless, but he is easily recognized by anyone in school from '59 to '63. The auto collision took place pretty much as described with one student dead and a young woman classmate severely injured. She was never compensated for her suffering because of an ugly piece of legislation known as the guest statute in effect in Ohio that plagued all plaintiffs who got into cars voluntarily knowing that the driver was intoxicated.

The "curse" or "hex" never occurred. The chapters recounting the Cancún murder and describing the lawyers supposedly affected by it are purely fictional. The incident involving the passed-over candidate during rush at the Sigma Chi house did occur, and I was president when the alums came down on us. Despite the pressure, the young man was never pledged. The rejection of my girlfriend as the Sigma Chi Sweetheart did occur, a hateful incident that had repercussions well into the future.

The rat story wasn't entirely made up. It was inspired by an incident in a ghastly Victorian cottage since refurbished on Peck Avenue on the Chautauqua grounds, which our family rented for one week during one summer. While using the toilet in the cottage, I noted that a large gray rat entered on one side of the bathroom and departed on the other after scurrying along the baseboard.

Later, my father, who had been alerted to the gray marauder's brazen appearance, noted blood beside the trap he had set under the kitchen stove. Later, my mother, while cooking there, looked down to see the wounded rat ascending her leg with teeth bared. Not a small woman, she jumped from that spot across the full length of the kitchen into my father's arms. He never forgot the experience.

My mother's screams alerted the upstairs tenant, who came down in time to relate a similar trauma she had experienced in the same cottage. While in her stocking feet, she stepped on a rat as she descended the main staircase at night.

About Rick Taylor

Author Rick Taylor grew up in the East End of Pittsburgh and graduated from Denison University, where he majored in English with an emphasis on writing. He authored several short stories before and after transitioning to writing legal briefs following his graduation from Pitt Law School. The writing bug never left him. In November 2022, he launched his first novel, *Curse of the Klondike*, which is described in detail on his website, readricktaylor.com.

His poetry has been featured in *Eureka*, the *Pittsburgh Post-Gazette*, the *California Quarterly*, and *Good News*, a Shepherdstown newspaper, and he has self-published three collections, including *Never Alone in a Cemetery*, *Headstone in the Headlights*, and *Musings Under a Buckboard*. In 2005, his poem "Foxfire" was awarded third place in the 2005 Penn Writers Poetry Contest.

www.ingramcontent.com/pod-product-compliance
Lightning Source LLC
LaVergne TN
LVHW041811060526
838201LV00046B/1218